The Family That Wasn't

A Novel

By Gene Twaronite

iUniverse, Inc.
New York   Bloomington

The Family That Wasn't
A Novel

This is a work of fiction. All of the characters, names, incidents, organizations, and dialogue in this novel are either the products of the author's imagination or are used fictitiously.

iUniverse books may be ordered through booksellers or by contacting:

iUniverse
1663 Liberty Drive
Bloomington, IN 47403
www.iuniverse.com
1-800-Authors (1-800-288-4677)

Because of the dynamic nature of the Internet, any Web addresses or links contained in this book may have changed since publication and may no longer be valid. The views expressed in this work are solely those of the author and do not necessarily reflect the views of the publisher, and the publisher hereby disclaims any responsibility for them.

ISBN: 978-1-4502-4517-3 (pbk)
ISBN: 978-1-4502-4518-0 (ebk)

Library of Congress Control Number: 2010911105

Printed in the United States of America

iUniverse rev. date: 8/24/10

Dedication: To my *real* family who will live inside me always

Acknowledgements

I wish to thank Josie, my wife and first reader, who by constructing the Boggle family tree included in this book helped me to see my characters in a new light. I also wish to thank my sister Maryanne (who is nothing at all like John's sister Venus—OK, maybe a little) for her thoughtful editorial suggestions. And a special thanks to photographer Josh Oakhurst for permission to use his photograph of an abandoned house in South Providence for the cover (the image has been modified from its original appearance). And last but not least, I wish to thank Publishing Services Associate Jade Council and other members of the Fitzgerald production team of IUniverse for patiently guiding me through the design process and helping to make this book a reality.

THE BOGGLE FAMILY TREE

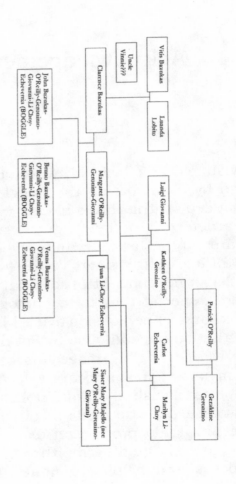

Vitis Baznikas

Luanda Lobito

Uncle Vinnie???

Clarence Baznikas

John Baznikas-O'Reilly-Geronimo-Giovanni-Li Choy-Echeverria (BOGGLE)

Bruno Baznikas-O'Reilly-Geronimo-Giovanni-Li Choy-Echeverria (BOGGLE)

Margaret O'Reilly-Geronimo-Giovanni

Luigi Giovanni

Kathleen O'Reilly-Geronimo

Venus Baznikas-O'Reilly-Geronimo-Giovanni-Li Choy-Echeverria (BOGGLE)

Juan Li-Choy Echeverria

Carlos Echeverria

Marilyn Li-Choy

Sister Mary Majello (nee Mary O'Reilly-Geronimo-Giovanni)

Patrick O'Reilly

Geraldine Geronimo

Chapter 1-The Boggle Curse

People lose families all the time. Sometimes it's a freak thing like a traffic accident or plane crash. And sometimes people just give up on each other through outright rejection or lack of interest. But you can never really lose your family completely. Even when they're gone they're still there inside you, for better or worse. And even if your old man is a complete jerk who beat you and your mother up every day and you haven't seen or talked to him for fifty years, there's still that memory you can't erase. He will go with you all the way to the grave.

But now I'm not so sure. You see, I didn't just lose my family. I wiped them out. I didn't mean to do it—things just got out of hand. One minute they were here—Dad and Mom, Bruno, Venus, Grandma Geronimo, Sister Mary and all the rest of my crazy family— and the next, they were gone, every last bit of them, gone as if they had never existed.

I am writing this down so I won't forget. I must *never* forget them. Did it really happen? Maybe I just made this all up in a dream. Have to admit, I do get carried away with my writing sometimes. But then, how do I explain what happened to Uncle Vinnie?

It all started with my name, John Boggle. Actually, it isn't really Boggle. That's just an acronym I invented to make life easier. My full name is John Bazukas-O'Reilly-Geronimo-Giovanni-Li Choy-Echeverria, or B.O.G.G.L.E. for short.

I remember crying a lot in first grade. While the other kids quickly learned how to write their names on their papers, I would begin to write John Bazukas, and sometimes make it to O'Reilly, but then get hopelessly lost. Finally, my principal, old Miss Vanderfield, wrote out the whole stupid thing for me on three long pieces of construction paper taped together, which I had to keep carrying around with me till I could remember how to write it. I felt like some creature in a zoo, stuck in a cage for everyone to look at, with a long Latin name printed over me.

Any one of these hyphenated names would have been all right with me. But no, my family had to go and have them all. How they ever managed to do this, and get together in the first place, is a tale far stranger than any I could ever imagine.

Chapter 2-The African-Lithuanian Connection

As far as I've been able to piece it together, I was born an African-Lithuanian-Irish-Apache-Italian-American, which was bad enough until my Chinese-Mexican stepfather decided to add his two cents worth.

The African-Lithuanian is from my dad's side—my *real* dad, that is. My grandfather, Vitis Bazukas, tired of the long cold winters in Lithuania, just took up and left his native country one day and headed south through Europe to the west coast of Africa. There he met and married my grandmother, a woman by the name of Luanda Lobito, who at the time was the acting chief of her village. Mom says the previous chief probably left to take a better paying job. Grandfather Vitis wanted her to take his last name, of course. But in her tribe it was the custom for the man to take the woman's name. To avoid an argument they both decided to just drop their last names and be known as Luanda and Vitis. Who needs a last name anyway?

For a time they lived happily in a little beach hut on the shore of the Atlantic. Just after my dad Clarence was born, however, Grandmother was attacked and eaten by a pack of rabid warthogs. Grandfather, who had been out grocery shopping, came home and found all that was left of her—a briefcase, assorted credit cards, and baseball cap—and little Clarence crying from under a zebra skin rug. Grandfather tracked down the warthogs and killed every last one of them, removing their tusks and tails, which he later sold to some tourists. Then, wrapping my dad in the zebra rug, he took the next ship to America.

Eventually, they made their way to Chicago, which though a lot colder than Africa had lots of both black and Lithuanian people living there. Grandfather, who was tall and very strong, got a job as a bouncer at a blues club, where my dad Clarence would spend the night asleep (or so Grandfather thought) on a cot in a back room.

After Grandfather lost his job during the Great Depression, they headed back East to Providence, Rhode Island. No one in the family knows really why they chose Providence. Maybe the name just sounded friendly. Anyway, there they settled along the shore of Narragansett Bay, where Grandfather took up life as a quahogger. (Quahog is the Narragansett Indian name for a kind of clam.)

My dad grew up with his father's love for music. Grandfather had taught him how to play the accordion by smell. Mom says he claimed that musical notes each had a unique smell that made a certain kind of brain wave in your head. He once knew a blind deaf-mute who could still play on his harmonica the sweetest tunes you ever heard. Dad bought a used ukulele at a Portuguese thrift shop in Fox Point, and he and Grandfather would often play together while sitting on the front stoop of their little shack on the bay.

When not helping Grandfather with the quahogging, Dad attended school and later worked as a music teacher and ukulele tuner. I never met Grandfather. He died from eating a bad quahog about a year before I was born. A few months later, Dad met my mother and things really started getting crazy.

Chapter 3-The Irish-Apache-Italian Connection

Mom's father, Luigi Giovanni, came over from Italy and, like many Italians before him, settled on Federal Hill, Providence, where he soon established the first combination pizza and funeral parlor in the country. It later grew into a whole chain of parlors, famous from coast to coast.

Early in his career, Grandfather Luigi met and married my grandmother, Kathleen O'Reilly-Geronimo, who worked for him as a pizza maker and occasional hearse driver. Because Grandma didn't want to give up her unique name, Grandpa just tacked on his own to make O'Reilly-Geronimo-Giovanni. But it was really Grandma's parents, my great grandparents, who started this hyphenated name business.

Her father, Patrick O'Reilly, had emigrated as a teenager from Ireland to Arizona in order to escape the Great Potato Famine. Finding the climate and scenery of southern Arizona to his liking, he decided that with a little irrigation it would make a good place to grow potatoes.

One day while in town, he met a young Apache woman putting up posters with the words, "U.S. Cavalry Go Home." Her name was Geraldine Geronimo, and she claimed to be a lost daughter of the great Apache chief. No one in the family can say for sure if this is true. Mom thinks she just liked the name Geronimo. Geraldine and Patrick fell in love and got married. However, since Geraldine wasn't about to give up her proud name for O'Reilly, they decided to keep both names. And so the Boggle curse was born.

For a while they tried farming potatoes, but soon grew tired of the cavalry always trampling their crop. They went up into the hills to join Geronimo, but never could quite find him. So they fought the cavalry on their own, putting up posters on every rock and cactus, and lobbing hot potatoes at passing troops. In the 1880's, things began getting too hot even for them (they had also run out of potatoes), so they fled Arizona and the cavalry and headed east to Providence, which they were told was a place where free thinkers were welcome. And it was there that my Grandma Kathleen was born.

While Grandma was in her teens, her parents suddenly headed back to Arizona—to join in the good fight, they said—and were never heard from again. Grandma says she can still see them there, throwing potatoes from some lonely purple butte, though both Geronimo and the cavalry are long gone.

At her last birthday, Grandma was 82 years old. She's the only real grandparent I ever knew. She's harmless, I guess, though sometimes she can be a real pain. Mostly she just works in the backyard, growing potatoes, or sits around telling stories about the land of Geronimo, which she still hopes to see someday before she dies. Over her long gray hair she wears a wide-brimmed wool hat with a red bandana wrapped around it. She wears it even in the bathtub. Her ruddy face reminds me of a cracked, dried up lake bottom. It's not easy to understand her because there's always a toothpick in her mouth, which she rolls around from one corner to the other as she talks.

I'm supposed to keep an eye on her, for you never know just where she'll end up. One time, I found her downtown at the Federal Building, sitting in the middle of the floor with a hundred anti-war protesters. She was shouting, "U.S. Cavalry Go Home!"

But back to Grandpa Luigi. During the Great Depression, his chain was wiped out (people were still dying, but nobody was buying pizza), and a few months later he died a broken man. Grandma Kathleen couldn't afford to live in their mansion on Federal Hill, so she and her two daughters, Margaret and Mary, moved to a small apartment in Fox Point.

To get over her grief and loneliness, Grandma started taking music lessons from my dad, who was also very lonely at the time, having just lost his father. Over the next few years, he and Grandma grew very close. And he couldn't help noticing as her daughters, especially Margaret, bloomed into young womanhood. But Grandma was very strict, and insisted that Dad wait until Margaret was seventeen before being allowed to court her. Several months later, they were married. And, yes, she too wanted to keep her proud name, though Dad insisted on putting his first. Mom's sister Mary, meanwhile, left to join a convent. So Mom and Grandma moved in with Dad to his little two-room shack on the bay.

It was there that my weird brother Bruno was born (more on him later) and, three years later, yours truly. I don't remember too much about those early days on the bay, but Bruno once told me about how the whole family used to sit out on the front stoop, singing and playing various instruments and waving at all the ships coming into port. Except for the sewage treatment plant next door, we pretty much had the shore all to ourselves.

When I was only two, Dad went away. He was sitting alone on the front stoop, playing his ukulele, right in the middle of a great hurricane. Mom had warned him to come inside, but as we watched helplessly he was carried away by the flood waters and swept down the bay out to sea. To this day I have this image of him bobbing in the foaming waves, still playing his ukulele. He was always talking about traveling to Africa and Lithuania some day. Perhaps he did.

After Dad left, there was little reason to stay by the bay, so we moved like a flock of pigeons to a new roost—an ugly, puke-green, two-story house in South Providence. The place is warped, cracked, and peeling, and appears to be dying. Someone should tear it down and put it out of its misery. The roof has been repaired so many times it looks like a patchwork quilt. The only part of the house I really like is the attic. At one end there's a small round window where you can look out over the city. I hang out up there a lot. As for our neighborhood, well, the nicest thing you can say about it is, at least we don't have a sewage treatment plant next door. There's plenty of garbage, though, along with loads of plump rats. And there's always something going on. Sirens blare day and night (the only time you ever notice them is when you don't hear them, which isn't very often). They say home is where the heart is. I just hope my heart finds a new place and soon.

Mom managed to get a job as a part-time sanitation worker for the City of Providence, the first woman ever to hold such a job. Though short and compact, she's got big hands and can throw garbage as well as any man. Every night when she comes home, she takes a bath and douses herself with cheap cologne. But she still smells like rotting fruit and coffee grounds.

About a year after we moved there, she met Juan, my so-called stepfather. Why she married the loser is beyond me. She might have at least waited another year or two for Dad to call ...

Chapter 4-The Chinese-Mexican Complication

It was all Bruno's fault. If he hadn't been performing experiments on our tropical fish, then Mom wouldn't have gone down to the pet shop to buy some more fish and meet Juan. My brother's always doing this kind of stuff. He says he wants to be a zoo veterinarian (specializing in parrots and marsupials). Three years ago, when I was just eight, he operated on all my stuffed animals one night. In the morning, I found all their heads had been transplanted from one to another. My teddy bear now had a zebra's head. My rhino had a crocodile head and so on. There were little patches all over them where he had removed some imaginary organ and replaced it with chicken livers or ravioli.

Later, when he got tired of stuffed animals, he began operating on real ones. We once had a parakeet, but after Bruno got through with it we had to put it to sleep. We should have put Bruno to sleep.

Bruno's middle initial is "K." It stands for Kathleen, which is supposed to be a secret but isn't. Mom had wanted a girl, so when Bruno was born she and Dad just named him Bruno K. on his birth certificate. Everyone in the universe, though, knows what the K. stands for. It's a good thing Bruno is 6 foot seven and 285 pounds.

This great ape and I have to share the same room. The only thing worse would be having my sister Venus as a roommate. It's bad enough Bruno plays on his accordion and electric bass zither all night, while singing the blues like a lovesick cow. (His other ambition is to be a musician. Fat chance.) But he also keeps these weird plants and animals all over the place, including a colony of giant Madagascar hissing cockroaches and a Kalahari kissing plant, which during the night attaches its sucker-like leaves to your lips to suck up the moisture. I always wake up in the morning with a dry mouth.

Anyway, as I started to explain, Mom had gone to the pet shop to buy some more tropical fish to replace the freaks that Bruno had created and which we had to flush down the toilet. The clerk who waited on her was a mouse-mannered guy with wire glasses, long gray ponytail, and a stupid looking handlebar mustache. His name was Juan Li Choy-

Echeverria. According to Mom, she fell in love with him on the spot while, with his head underwater and with too small a net, he tried to corner a wily zebra danio. Finally, gasping for breath, his net still empty, he raised his head out of the tank and asked her in a gentle voice, "How about a guppy, instead?" They were married a few weeks later.

At this moment Juan is employed as an epoxy painter at a local jewelry factory. Before that he was assistant manager at a convenience store. By his count this makes a grand total of 200 different jobs he's held. He's forever babbling about the unique flavor of each job, as if slopping hamburgers or sweeping floors were somehow special. Too bad he couldn't be more like his rich parents, who I'm supposed to call grandparents but don't.

His Mexican father, Carlos Echeverria, met his Chinese mother, Marilyn Li Choy (named after Marilyn Monroe), while working as migrant artichoke pickers in southern California. Both proud of their heritages, they too became a hyphenated couple. After saving a little money, they settled down in Bakersfield, where Juan was born. There they opened up a small cactus nursery that soon grew into Li Choy-Echeverria Cactus Growers, Inc., a multi-million dollar company that now supplies landscape plants to all the bone-dry cities of the Southwest. They live in a big condo with a cactus-shaped swimming pool, somewhere near San Diego.

I don't see them much, which is a good thing because all they ever do is talk about cacti. Once, they visited us in their silver Mercedes. Didn't stay long, though. I guess they don't like our neighborhood all that much.

Juan headed East right after high school. He says he didn't know what he wanted to do except to get away from anything that looked like a cactus. For ten years he zigzagged across the country, hitchhiking and taking odd jobs. Mom calls him her little road runner. He claims that he's ready to settle down here in Providence, but I don't believe him. There's something funny about a guy who looks at maps all the time. I say good riddance, if he does leave.

When not drooling over maps, he's writing in that dopey book of his. His job book, he calls it. Every time he gets a new job, he writes all about it. You'd think he was just elected president or something the way he goes on, but all it is is just another crummy job at a factory or store. I took a peek at it once, but everything was in either Spanish or Chinese, as if he doesn't want anyone else to read it. Who would *want* to read it?

Shortly after Mom married Juan, my half sister Venus was born. Wanting a good classical name and both being a little mushy headed, my folks decided to call her Venus

Margaret, after the mythological Goddess of Love and my dear silly mother.

Goddess of love, my ass! The little nut's infatuated with the planet Venus. That's all she ever talks or dreams about. She actually believes she'll go there someday. Worse, she thinks it's inhabited by beautiful, pale-skinned people who wear long white robes lined with strange, colorful flowers and speak only in rhyming verse. She's even got her own club, the Blackstone Valley Venusians Society, of which she's the president and only member so far.

It's not easy having a Venusian for a sister. Sometimes she covers her face with white powder and puts on white bed sheets, with pictures of flowers taped all over them. It would be all right if she just stayed in the house where no one could see her. But then, dressed up like a flowery ghost and chewing a clove of garlic (which is supposed to be the chief food of the Venusians), she decides to tag along after me. I'll be walking down the street and someone will yell, "Hey, look! It's John and the Venusian." I try to just look the other way, but when guys start pushing her around and tearing her sheets, well, she is my half sister. I have to do something. Normally I don't get into fights—there's usually a way out if you just use your head—but the Venusian has got me into some real doozies. Once I even got my nose broken. It's still a little crooked and smarts whenever I look at her.

Despite all this, Mom says Venus has a genius I.Q. She's always reading books about calculus, quantum mechanics, astrophysics, and philosophy—just for fun, she claims. But how can anyone that smart be dumb enough to believe in Venusians? And how come I got stuck with her...and with this whole crazy family?

Chapter 5-A Family Farce

I sometimes think I could learn to accept my family if only they didn't keep on getting worse. But, day after day, they're forever inventing new ways to astound me. Like players on a stage, they go from one silly scene to another, acting out a drama that makes no sense at all. Though forced into being a player myself at times, mostly I just sit and watch in disbelief.

As if things weren't bad enough, some new players have recently been added to the cast. Sister Mary Majello, for instance, Mom's older sister. She just moved in with us after her convent was converted to condominiums. She belongs to a religious order called the Sisters of Creation, who believe that all creatures— including rats, cockroaches and even rock musicians—are created equal in God's eyes and deserve the same rights and respect as people, or perhaps more so in the case of some people. All dressed in black, with a pair of bifocals perched on her long sharp nose and a silver medal on her chest which shows a dog with its paws folded in prayer and a halo over its head, she's one scary bird. With her shrill voice and bony fingers, Sister Majello's always preaching and pointing at us during dinner. She'll tell us to pray for the termites, or to do penance for all the microbes we've swallowed today. I don't know why she's always on my case. A strict vegetarian, she keeps telling me that I'm going straight to hell for eating meat and wearing leather shoes. Not exactly my favorite person in the world.

I'd gladly put up with ten of her, though, in place of the newest player in our family, "Uncle" Vinnie. I'm not even sure if he is a member of our family. He just showed up at our doorstep one day, holding his suitcase and introducing himself as Grandfather Vitis's nephew from Lithuania. Though there was no family record of Vitis ever having a nephew named Vinnie, Mom simply asked him if he could speak Lithuanian—which he could—and of course that was proof enough for her. Just like that he became a member of our household. "Family is family," Mom says.

Everybody just started calling him Uncle Vinnie. He's a squatty little man with a round pasty face, gray crew cut hair and a veiny bulbous nose (which, though big as mine, doesn't look one bit like a Bazukas nose). And he's forever bragging about how strong he is.

"Feel muscle," he will say, flexing his arm in my face. "Like mountain." I once saw him lift up one end of the family car so that Juan could change the tire.

He says he's still looking for the right job and a good sturdy wife who will cook, wash, and sew for him and keep his feet warm in the winter. Good luck. Mom doesn't do any of those things for Juan. All she knows is garbage. It's a good thing Juan can cook, at least.

Uncle Vinnie claims to have been a great sports hero at the Vilnius Academy in Lithuania, where he earned letters in ice hockey, rugby, and cabbage throwing. He's always bugging me about going out for football, boxing or other manly sports. In fact, he's always got his big fat nose into everybody's business but his own. One minute, he'll be complaining about how women are getting "too uppity" and how a wife should always take her husband's last name because "it says so in the Bible." The next thing, he'll be making fun of Juan's latest job or telling me that "only sissies write in books."

Mostly I try to ignore him, but it's not easy. He just hangs around the house, reading Lithuanian newspapers and smoking cigars that smell like burnt wood pulp. Always criticizing everyone and everything, he's the ugliest person I've ever known. Have to admit, he scares me sometimes. I wish he would just go away. One day I caught his dog Pragaras (which is Lithuanian for "hell") up in my room, eating one of my books. But when I complained to Uncle Vinnie, he just chortled, then stared at me with his cold blue eyes and said, "Lucky it only dumb book. He used to have couple boys like you for breakfast. But I train him good. Now he eat other things." Then he just laughed and squeezed my nose so hard it was red for a week.

One day, however, my family scene became so unreal that I just couldn't take it anymore. We were all sitting at the dinner table (assembled from three rickety card tables Mom had "rescued" from the streets) and staring at Juan's latest dish—tofu and peanut butter enchiladas with noodles—when one of the enchiladas began to walk off the platter across the table.

Uncle Vinnie slammed his fist down, splattering tofu and peanut butter everywhere.

"You've killed my roach!" screamed Bruno.

"Serve him right, said Uncle Vinnie, tossing the four-inch bug at Sister Majello. "Here, go bury corpse."

"Poor little thing," said Sister Majello, wrapping the squashed roach in her napkin. "Mark my words, Vinnie, you'll roast in hell for this."

21

Uncle Vinnie just snorted, then looked across the table at Juan. "What you writing now?" he asked.

"Oh, I'm just jotting down some notes on my last job," said Juan. "Don't mind me. Go ahead and eat."

"What you mean, *last* job?" demanded Uncle Vinnie. "Great Perkunas! You no lose new one?"

"Just for now," said Juan in a calm voice. "I'll get another tomorrow. I thought I might try being a telemarketer for a while. You get to talk on the phone to all kinds of interesting people. It should be fun."

"Not again!" said Mom. "You were only at the jewelry factory for two weeks. How are we going to pay the bills if you don't find work?" Then, shrugging her shoulders, she dumped the contents of a big duffel bag out onto the table. "Well, at least we won't starve. Look what I've found in today's garbage. It's amazing what people throw away."

There spread before us were Mom's proud gifts to her family: half of a salami with chew marks at one end; a slightly dusty and very smelly anchovy pizza; ten completely different shoes and sneakers; a twisted and mangled umbrella; two cans of used tennis balls; and about two thousand wire coat hangers. "Someday, I'll invent a good use for these hangers and we'll all be stinkin' rich," she proclaimed.

As I watched, a scout party of Bruno's Madagascar hissing roaches carried the anchovy pizza away. "I think I've lost my appetite." I was just about to get up from the table when in walked Venus in her full Venusian getup.

"I have a brief announcement to make, dear family. On this very night I have successfully made contact with a Venusian scientist by the name of Dr. Valvar. Laugh all you want, but after tonight I will no longer be the butt of your jokes. Dr. Valvar is making all the necessary arrangements, and at precisely 7:45 tomorrow morning I will leave you all to go live on the planet Venus. Sorry, but that's the way it is." And with that she sat down next to me and started chewing her garlic.

"How long you put up with this little cabbage head?" asked Uncle Vinnie, his mouth stuffed with enchilada and noodles.

"If Venus wants to believe in Venusians, that's fine," said Mom. "At least she believes in *something*."

That's another thing about this family—everybody is supposed to believe in something. We've had more different religions and beliefs in this family than programs on TV. We're always flipping the channels, going from astrology to Zoroastrianism, and everything in between. Mom and Juan both insist that we should try them all so we'll know which one is best. I hope we can settle on one before I grow up.

"And as long as we're making announcements," Mom continued, "I'd like to make one myself. You boys are going to have to share a room with Uncle Vinnie. I need your room to store my recyclables. We'll move your beds tonight. Sorry, boys."

Uncle Vinnie turned toward me and grinned. "Must get more books for Pragaras. Not want him eating boys tonight."

I was so mad I couldn't even talk. It wasn't just losing our room to garbage or, worse, moving in with Uncle Vinnie. It was everything! This time, my family had gone too far. Like a mad dog, it was foaming at the mouth.

I shoved away from the table and raced upstairs, seeking refuge in the only sane place in the house, my writing room in the attic. In my ears was the distant sound of Bruno's bellowing and the silly rhyme that Venus was singing:

From this earthly vail of sorrow
I will leave you all tomorrow.
Look to the West and you'll see us—
Me and my friends on planet Venus.

And that was the last I remembered of my stupid family.

Chapter 6-An Ideal Family

My "writing room" is actually a corner of the attic, next to the small round window. There I can look out past the boarded up houses and weedy, trashy streets to the city skyline and beyond, to the faraway places I dream of. Set upon my mahogany writing table (all right, so it's only a couple of crates and a plank of pine wood that I found at the dump) is the big green journal where I travel. I live in its pages whenever life gets too dull or too crazy, or just plain impossible.

For a few minutes, I just stared at the next blank page and wondered how to begin. This time, the view through the window was no help. Neither were my bookshelves (more planks of wood on cinder blocks), lined with dog-eared books of travel, legends and adventure. Finally, it dawned on me that it wasn't a new place I needed to write about, but a new family.

As I gazed at the top shelf, a title from one of the reference books caught my eye— *Bartlett's Familiar Quotations*. Right next to it was my old worn copy of *The Wizard of Oz* by L. Frank Baum. Suddenly the way was clear, and I began to write a new and improved life story...

My name is John Bartlett, I wrote, and I live in an ivy-covered mansion on College Hill in Providence. I am an only child, with a perfect nose, a perfect family, and a perfect life.

My father is L. Frank Bartlett. I guess I'm lucky his name isn't John; that would have made me John Bartlett II, which sounds kind of wimpy. I like my name just the way it is. It's a good, respectable, all American name ... and easy to spell.

Father says the Bartletts trace their roots through fourteen generations, all the way back to England. He says I've definitely got the Bartlett nose—a proud but sensible nose that doesn't call attention to itself. We Bartletts don't need to flaunt our good looks and success. We've had brilliant inventors, scientists, doctors, senators, company presidents, and even a duke or two. There are no losers in our family.

Father's a self-made man who has always known exactly what he wanted to do in life, which is to invent new and useful words. Words such as "grozzle," "hyrovia," and, my favorite, "proplumpadiddly." People often wonder how new words get added to dictionaries. It's because creative people like my father are inventing them, that's how. Each day, he goes up to his study and tinkers away at his word synthesizer, trying out fresh new combinations of letters and sounds. When finally, after much hard work, he's discovered a good meaty word that seems to have possibilities, he gives it one last polish and sends it out to any one of a number of word publishers around the country. The publisher then decides whether the word has merit and, of course, what it will actually mean (which is far less important, really, than how it sounds). For each word they buy, publishers pay Father an advance—usually at least $10,000 or more—and then a royalty payment for every time that word is used by anyone in the world. Father's always being interviewed by reporters. He's probably one of the greatest wordsmiths who ever lived. What's more, he makes tons of money at it.

A graduate of Brown University, Father sometimes teaches a course there in word construction. He's not one of those stuffy professor types, though. He always seems perfectly comfortable with himself and whatever he's doing, whether it's lecturing, sailing, or playing polo. Six feet tall and built like an athlete, he moves with the grace of a gazelle and the confidence of a lion. Though smart, he's never flashy about it. I can't remember him ever yelling at me or anyone. In a calm, clear voice he just tells you what he expects of you or how he feels about things. He's friendly and knows how to laugh, though he never gets carried away with it. But he never cries, for why should he? He's got everything a man could want in life.

Complementing him perfectly is my beautiful mother, Roberta J. Bartlett. Born Roberta Judith Williams, she's a direct descendant of Roger Williams, founder of Providence. She met Father at an English conference in Boston, where he was giving a lecture on word composition. Smitten by one of his new words—"floove"—she flooved for him, as she put it, and wrote a poem about her feelings entitled, "A Fool for Floove." An accomplished poet, Mother has written well over a thousand different poems. None of them has yet been published. Most are about flowers, sunsets, romance, and tennis. She writes them for her own amusement. To make money from poetry is just too unladylike, she insists.

A junior at Wellesley College at the time, Mother decided to drop out and marry Father. He calls her "my little elf queen." A pale-skinned, delicate woman with soft green eyes, long golden hair, tiny hands and trim waist, she does seem at times too beautiful for this world. She is happiest when sitting in the sun room, writing a new poem, or singing to herself while gardening in our large backyard, filled with flowers and statues of fairy tale characters.

Her full-time career, she says, is simply making Father and me happy. Though she is active in several clubs, including the East Side Garden Club and the Providence Beautification Committee, and enjoys playing tennis, she is always there for us when we need her. She is everything a mother should be. She even smells good.

One of the things I love most about our little family is that I don't have to share it with anyone. My parents give me all their love and undivided attention. I never have to worry about pesky brothers and sisters, or nosy relatives moving in with us. What few relatives I know of all seem perfectly normal and keep their proper distance, while the ones I don't know are smart enough to stay that way. Mother's parents, Robert and Judith Williams, are just right. They live in Florida and occasionally visit us in their Jaguar. Actually, I wouldn't mind seeing them more often because they always bring me nice, thoughtful gifts. Last year, they gave me a big TV for my room. This year, they've promised to take me on a month-long safari to Africa. And when I turn sixteen, they're going to buy me a sports car. A guy couldn't ask for better grandparents.

***

Reading over what I had just written, I smiled and shouted to myself, "*Yes!*" For it all sounded so real, so right. Then I gazed through the window of my well-furnished room. It was a picture perfect view. Ivy-colored towers and church steeples, stately Victorian houses with slate roofs, all in perfect repair, and right below, a private backyard garden filled with flowers and fairy tale statues. A beautiful young woman with long golden hair was singing softly to herself as she weeded. She turned her head to look up at me and waved.

I waved back at her, then closed my journal and went downstairs.

Chapter 7-A New Life

As I walked down the marble stairs, the familiar paintings of my illustrious Bartlett ancestors greeted me. There was my great-great grandfather, Phinneas T. Bartlett, one of the most famous brain surgeons in the country. And Captain Felix M. Bartlett, my uncle, who was killed in the Great War while taking out a machine gun nest. There, too, smiling from a large oil portrait at the bottom of the stairs, was a representative from my mother's side—Roger Williams, founder of Providence.

"John, where have you been?" said a sweet voice from the sun room. "Have you forgotten about the party tonight? All your relatives are so looking forward to seeing you. Please make sure to wear your best suit—the blue one, OK?" Mother put down her notebook and placed her dainty hand on my head. "Were you upstairs again, John?"

"Yes, Mother. I was just jotting down some notes about our family. I'm sure to find something there for a story ... eventually."

"Oh, splendid idea!" said Mother. "Perhaps I should do the same. I've been trying all afternoon to write this poem entitled 'Ode to a Food Processor,' but it's just not going well, I'm afraid. Anyway, it's time for tea. Would you like some, John? I have some of your favorite imported cookies."

"No thanks, Mother. I just needed to take a short break. Think I'll go for a walk."

"You work much too hard at your writing, dear. I wish you would relax more. Get out and have some fun. You know what they say. Writing is 5 percent inspiration and 95 percent relaxation. You have to feel good to write well."

"Yes, Mother. I'll see you in a little while."

"Don't forget about the dinner party, John. Make sure you're back before six."

Closing the arched oak door behind me, I drifted down Power Street, then moseyed right on Benefit, with no particular destination in mind. Near the Rhode Island School of Design campus, I ducked as a Frisbee sailed over my head from a group of art students playing on the grass. Maybe I should drop in on my friend, Preston Phillips, and check out his new stereo system. Or go wander through the dimly lit stacks of the Athenaeum, where Edgar Allen Poe once roamed. Then, too, there was always the museum or art cinema. There were hundreds of things to do. But instead I headed up College Hill toward Thayer Street, where something was always happening.

The college students milling about reminded me that in just five more years I, too, would be attending Brown University, just like Father. Unlike Father, however, I planned to major in creative writing.

In a store window was the racing bike I'd been planning to buy with this week's allowance. It's what I'd always wanted, or at least since last week when I first saw it. Maybe I should just wait and let my grandparents buy it, though.

I wandered about some more, like a cruise liner in a sea of contentment, then suddenly realized it was almost six and headed for home. Our great house, built in 1798 by a sea captain, was all lit up, as if to tell everyone on the street that we were having another party.

As the door slammed shut behind me, I could hear its echo down the long, mahogany-paneled hallway.

"Is that you, son?" said Father. The door to his study was open. I went in and found him sitting in his red leather chair and smoking his pipe. He was wearing his usual tweed jacket, vest and bow tie. A ring of smoke hung over his handsome gray head, which was tilted in deep reflection.

"So what have you been up to?" he asked. "Mother says you were up in your room most of the afternoon."

"Yes, Father. I was catching up on my homework," I lied. There was no sense in upsetting him before dinner.

"That's my boy. It's a hard world out there and, sad to say, you'll need more than our family's name and good looks to get into college. By the way, have you thought anymore about what you'll major in at Brown?"

"I'd like to be a writer, so ..."

"You don't want to be a writer, John. Don't get me wrong. We need writers to inform and entertain us. I mean, *somebody* has to do it. But that's not where the real money is. Take it from your father, a wordsmith is what you want to be. Invent a better word and the world will be at your door. Now, I was just looking through this catalog and I think that a combined major in phonics and economics would be just right for you. What do you think?"

"I know you and Mother only want the best for me, but I think I'd still like to be a writer."

"You know, I'm beginning to wonder if we haven't been too patient with you on this writing thing of yours," said Father, in his sternest voice. "We bought you that electric typewriter so that you could put it to constructive use. We've never begrudged you using it on your little writing hobby, just as long as it didn't hurt your studies. Why, look at Mother. You don't see her running off to be a poet. She knows where poetry ends and life begins. But it's time you face reality, young man. Words are for making money, not for make-believe. Now go upstairs and get ready for the party."

"Yes, Father." What could I say? He was definitely not in the mood for further discussion. On my way out, I gazed again at all his plaques and trophies, reminding me of how proud I was to have such a famous father. But why couldn't he understand me?

"Oh, and one more thing," said Father. "It's about time you went out for the polo team next year. All the Bartletts play polo. It's a fine, manly sport. You'll like it."

Chapter 8-Writer's Block

I put on the blue suit that I always wear to these parties, then sat down at my desk. Dinner wouldn't be served until all our relatives had arrived and, besides, I wanted Churchill, our butler, to have to come up and get me. I love the way Churchie scowls and says, "Sir, your faaawwther and mother await you in the main dining room."

Still stuck on just how to begin, I flipped through my journal again. It was full of jolly good stuff about my family and friends, and the wonderful life I lead. There was the month we visited all the national parks in the country, spending a full fifteen minutes in each one. Or the time we bought a new house in Connecticut, but then decided to stay in Providence after all—boy, was that ever exciting! Why, there was even a list of all the interesting foods I'd eaten during the past two years. Obviously, I had plenty of things to write about. All I needed was a fresh new angle or gimmick, and everything would fall into place.

Just then, there was a curt rap at the door.

"Be right down, Churchie." I closed my journal and went down to join my family. Maybe I would find some inspiration there.

The party had just begun. Grandfather Williams came over and gave me a pat on the head. Then he pulled me aside and put an envelope in my hands. "It's for that bike you wanted," he whispered, smiling. "Our little secret."

Before I could thank him, he rushed off with Grandmother to the other side of the room to sample some new little appetizers the cook had invented.

A hard slap on my back told me that Cousin Filbert was here, too. He was usually a lot of fun and I enjoyed hanging out with him, but sometimes he said stuff just to piss me off.

"How's life, Johnnie boy? You still want to be a writer?" he asked, with a jackass grin. "You know, lots of famous people are writers. Of course, most of them are dead." For some reason this struck him as enormously funny. I was just about to say something when Mother announced that dinner was ready to be served.

I sat down at my usual place, right next to the stuffed hippopotamus. That was Uncle Ferdinand's idea. He had once been a big game hunter, but had given it up because he'd run out of new and different animals to shoot. "Every house should have a hippo," he was always saying. I liked him a lot—the hippo, I mean.

We all bowed our heads as Father said grace:

> *Thank you, oh Lord, for this food we eat*
> *And a perfect life that can't be beat.*
> *And thank you for this fine family*
> *That you made so fantabulously.*

Then we began to feast. There was plenty of the usual fare—filet mignon, lobster, caviar, pheasant under glass and poached salmon—as well as many welcome surprises such as pickled ostrich eggs, kangaroo liver pâté, and stir-fried sea horses. At our house eating was always an adventure.

As I finished my dessert of deviled plum pudding, Aunt Florence asked me about my plans for the summer. I told her that I was planning to travel with my grandparents, then just hang around, I suppose, at our beach cottage, Cliffside Manor in Watch Hill. I also told her that I hoped to do some writing, if time permitted.

"At your age I think it high time that you learned some social graces, my boy. The way you handled that spoon and slurped your plum pudding is positively disgraceful! We Bartletts must set an example for the world.

Your mother and I have been talking, and we've both decided that you should spend this summer at an etiquette camp in the Catskills. You'll learn not only how to eat, how to sit, and how to talk, but how to think properly. They'll make a gentleman out of you yet, though of course we do love you just the same, in spite of your bad habits. But you're thirteen years old, John. You can't just go on doing what you please. This writing business is a pleasant enough diversion, but there are far more important things in life. You'll thank us for this someday. Now give your Aunt Florence a nice big kiss. John ...? Well, I never! A gentleman would at least have the decency to excuse himself from the table."

"Go kiss yourself, you old poop!" I muttered to myself, slamming the door to my room. "What does she know about important? Who cares about which spoon to use?" Then I laughed and turned on my typewriter. Nobody took Aunt Florence too seriously. And if things get sticky, I knew I could just ask Grandmother to intervene. Now where was I?

Oh yes, I was trying to write. I stared at the empty white page. For a minute or so, I really tried to think, then found my brain idling again over pleasant distractions. "Boy, wasn't that pudding good tonight?" I thought, smacking my lips. "And I can't wait to go buy that bike. Wait till Preston sees it. He'll ... All right, enough of that. Back to work. Why does writing have to be so hard?"

I ran my fingers over my new typewriter. It was the fastest, most advanced machine that money could buy. Voice activated, it would respond to my every word. I just had to speak into a microphone and my thoughts would come pouring onto the page. All that power to create, just waiting to be unleashed. All I had to do was come up with an idea.

Suddenly I felt something, a strange uneasiness deep inside me. I loosened my tie and belt. Could this be the inspiration I was waiting for? My guts were twitching uncontrollably now as I stared at the screen. Then I belched. It was only indigestion.

For a few more minutes I sat there, gazing at the empty page, then turned off the machine.

"What's the matter with me? I've always been able to write before ... or have I?"

I walked over to my dresser and looked into the mirror. It was the same good-looking face I remembered, right down to the perfect Bartlett nose. Hmmm. Maybe too perfect. All of a sudden, my nose seemed like an odd, funny thing, like some alien attachment.

It was the same with my room. There all around me were the things I knew and loved, or at least I thought I did. My solid mahogany writing desk and swivel chair. My library of over two thousand books, with their bright leather spines. Even the full-size model of a Tyrannosaurus skull in a glass case. There was nothing out of order. No dust or dark corners. Nothing that could be improved. It all seemed too good to be true. It was a perfect picture, as perfect as if I had made it all up. The thought hit me like a ton of wet garbage.

"That's crazy!" I yelled at the mirror. "How could I not be who I am?" I hit the side of my head as if my ears were clogged with water. But the thought would not go away. I stared again at the mirror. It was the image of a stranger. "But if I'm not who I am, then who am I? And why can't I write?"

In vain I looked around at my books for answers, but they were no help. Like all the other perfect things in my room, they suddenly seemed mere props with no connections to the past. In vain I tried to remember the exact occasions when I had acquired them. I went to the window and stared past the steeples and houses of the East Side, to the bright city lights of downtown Providence and beyond. Then, closing the door behind me, I crept down the stairs.

Fortunately, the party was over and all our relatives had left. I could hear Mother in the kitchen, singing a French ballad. Father, as always, was in his den. It was a good thing, too, for he would have demanded to know just where I was going at that hour, with a knapsack on my back. I couldn't tell

41

him, of course, mainly because I didn't know myself.

Closing the front door with a sad thunk, I slipped silently off into the night.

Chapter 9-The Dead House

The full moon bathed the streets in a fairy glow. The stately mansions of my neighborhood seemed like houses of a strange and distant kingdom. Inside them there were warm lights shining, with people living and dreaming, but to me they might as well have been on another planet. And the biggest house of all, one that I called home, now seemed sadly empty, though I couldn't say why. I felt like a traveler, trying to imagine myself actually living there, once.

Unlike most travelers, however, I didn't have the slightest clue of my destination. All I knew was that I had to get away from that big house on Power Street.

For awhile, out of habit, I headed back down Benefit Street over to Fox Point. Past Wickenden Street, I could see the gray outlines of gas tanks by the bay. And beyond them, I knew, was the strange land of Sassafras Point, where the sewage treatment plant was and God knows what else. Why I should be thinking about that awful place I could not say. Nice people just don't go there, certainly not a Bartlett. But still, there was something about that place that made me all squirmy inside.

The festive lights of Point Street Bridge beckoned me to follow them across the dark mirror of the Providence River, where the city skyline stretches across the water. I followed Point Street, then took a left on Eddy Street, which eventually led me under Interstate 95 into a part of South Providence. I knew I was somewhere just west of the harbor, but why had I come here? This was not exactly the best place to go strolling around at night. The newspapers were full of its daily life—murder, muggings, and other stuff you don't want to know. As I stood there, a police siren blared from the next street over. A person would have to be crazy to want to live there, and I was beginning to wonder if I wasn't crazy myself. For instead of heading straight back to my safe and high home on College Hill, I spent the next couple of hours wandering this maze of dark streets, searching for who knows what.

Finally, I came to a house that looked more miserable than all the rest. Though all the street lamps were broken, I could see from the light of the moon that it was a sickly green. Part of the roof was caved in, and all the windows were boarded up. There were bullet holes along one wall. Obviously no one had lived there for a very long time. It was a dead house.

I don't know why, but something about that dumb house pulled me toward it like a buzzard to a carcass. Before I could stop myself, I had pried off a loose board from one window and climbed inside.

Moonlight spilled down through the hole in the roof, revealing a flight of stairs. As I made my way up them, a huge rat scurried past me. I jumped and cursed myself for being there. Yet still I kept going, all the way up to the attic.

There, in one corner, I found a round window. Next to it was a wooden plank set upon two cinder blocks. And on the plank was a big green book, covered with cobwebs.

Pulling a penlight out of my knapsack, I sat down on the floor and began to flip through the book. The pages were all discolored and brittle with age, and hard to read. It seemed to be some kind of journal. On the front page were the words, "Written by John B.O.G.G.L.E." The name leaped out at me. I found myself saying it aloud over and over again in the darkness. What *was* it about that name? (And why were there periods after each letter of the last name?) This Boggle fellow had written a lot about some crazy family, which must have been all made up because no family could be that crazy. There were also observations, mostly made while looking through this

45

window, as well as various stories and poems about faraway places. The little that I could make out sounded vaguely familiar, almost as if I had read them someplace before. Then I read the last few pages, which began:

> My name is John Bartlett, and
> I live in an ivy-covered mansion
> on College Hill in Providence. I
> am an only child, with a perfect
> nose, a perfect family, and a
> perfect life ...

"No, it can't be!" I shouted. Shaking all over, I slammed the book shut. "It's absurd! My name is ..." I grabbed for the book again. But as I did so, its pages all crumbled into dust.

I flew down the stairs and out of that awful house. Then I ran and I ran, down one street after another, trying to erase that which would not go away.

But it was no use. I could not hide from the impossible truth. My name is John Boggle, and I have written my family away. And that is all I really knew, except that somehow or other I must get them back.

Chapter 10-The Quest

Can't say how I got there, but I awoke to find myself riding in the cab of a trailer truck carrying Rhode Island quahogs to Florida. It was 3 a.m. We were on Interstate 95, somewhere in New Jersey, I think, though it could have been anywhere. All highways look the same at that hour, all part of that same magic landscape of streaming headlights, glowing signs, and the ever unrolling carpet of asphalt. Nothing is real but the open road.

The truck driver, with a cigar in her mouth and wearing a sailor's watch cap, was singing along with the radio. She had the smell of the sea at low tide. Like a sea captain, she talked mostly of all the voyages she had taken with her great wheeled ship.

Then I told her my story, and she listened without saying a word. She just nodded occasionally, looking over at me with misty brown eyes.

"So there you have it," I said. "Am I crazy or what?"

"You know," she said, "when I stopped to pick you up back in Providence, you were one sad character. I just knew you were running away from something. We all are, in one way or another. The trick is in finding out what it is, so you can get on with running *to* something as well. Or, in your case, back to something you've lost."

"But how can I ever find my family again? They're all gone. There's nothing left but a dead house. I can't even remember what they look like, or who I really am."

"They're not really gone, John. Our families live inside us, sort of like characters in a story. But if you stop believing, and close the book on them, the family ceases to exist. I, too, once had a family, a long time ago it seems. And, just like you, I wrote them out of my life. Maybe someday I'll find them again." For a few minutes the driver stared silently through the windshield, almost as if she were trying to see someone out there.

"But where do I start?"

"You've already started your quest. You've realized that you need them in order to be who you are. All you must do now is to believe enough to make them real again. They're still there, somewhere deep inside you. Try seeing them through new eyes, not only as they were but as they hope to be. You say that you're a writer, John. If you wish to bring them back, you must recreate their story."

At dawn, the driver pulled off at a donut shop in Delaware. I decided it was time to head off on my own. I asked her which way she would go, for as far as I knew my family could be anywhere.

"That's easy," she said. "I'd go west, of course—the Great Faraway West. For no matter where I travel, in my heart I'm always headed that way. Everything's bigger than life out there—mountains, trees, animals, and even people. It's a land where anything seems possible ... where a person can breathe free and go for the stars, and be anything she wants to be." She grinned and gave me a bag of donuts.

Then, thanking her, I strapped on my trusty knapsack and began walking westward. For now, it was as good a direction as any.

I journeyed for days on end, sleeping under the open sky on park benches or forest floors. All I had to eat were donuts. But they were the most amazing donuts I'd ever eaten. I never grew tired of them, for they tasted different each time, and just one was enough for a full day's travel. And though I was sure the driver had given me only half a dozen, the bag was never empty.

In each town or city through which I passed, my first stop was a phone booth. There I'd scan the directory for the name Boggle. But it was always the same. There would be Biggles and Bigelows, even Bungles and Bagels, but no Boggles. It was if no one with that name had ever existed.

But, if not through my name, how else could I find my family? It would be nice if they had just left me a big road sign: "This way to the Lost Family." Still, there must be some kind of sign I could look for. I thought again about the truck driver and her gift of donuts. What was it she had said—something about things "bigger than life" and where "anything might be possible?" Maybe she was trying to give me a clue.

I crossed the Mississippi and wandered clear across the Great Plains. I even wandered underground through the Meramec Caverns of Missouri, but all I found there were bat droppings and a stalagmite shaped like Elvis Presley. And, in the ancient fossil beds of Dinosaur National Monument in Colorado, all I could see were skeletons of loving and happy dinosaur families, now extinct.

Then, just outside of Las Vegas, Nevada, I saw a huge sign on the horizon. In flashing colored lights it read: "Four Winds Palace. Fun for the Whole Family." There was a picture of a young woman in a bikini playing a slot machine shaped like a cactus. I stared at the sign and wondered. It did seem like fun and the sign was pretty big. But was it bigger than life? I decided not and headed south into Arizona.

There I found a number of things that did at least seem bigger than life. There was Grand Canyon, whose sprawling emptiness almost swallowed me up, where I rode the rapids of the mighty Colorado River on a large piece of driftwood, shaped like a ukulele. Bobbing in the white water dimly reminded me of something terrible that had happened long ago. Try as I might, though, I couldn't remember what it was, only that it made me feel more alone than ever.

And there was the Petrified Forest—a forest of dead things—where I found a giant section of log that looked just like a petrified pepperoni pizza. It, too, seemed bigger than life, but what could such a thing possibly mean?

Though I saw many such curiosities and wonders, after several more weeks of travel I was beginning to doubt if I would ever find my family. It was 3 a.m. again. The cool night air felt good after a long hot march in the desert sun. Just east of Phoenix, I entered a small town, with palm trees and huge cacti lining the streets. Too tired to even notice what its name was, I stumbled into a small, cheap-looking motel and plunked down my last few dollars for a much needed rest in a real bed. The room was a mess. The bed was unmade, and there were splotches of unwholesome-looking substances covering the walls and floor. But, for some reason, it made me feel right at home. In no time at all I was fast asleep and didn't wake up until almost noon.

Chapter 11-Geronimo!

I awoke to a hard knock at the door. "Come on, open up, you lazy bum," said a croaky voice. "I haven't got all day, you know. You're supposed to be out of here."

Jumping out of bed, I opened the door and greeted a wrinkly old man in tattered cowboy hat. He was holding a scrub brush and bucket of disinfectant. "It's about time!" he said.

"What town am I in?" I asked, rubbing the sleep from my eyes.

"Don't you know nuthin'? This is Apache Junction, gateway to miles and miles of worthless desert and the Superstition Mountains, where you can spend your entire fool life following stupid legends. I should know. Sixty years and what have I got to show for it? A good suntan and a two-bit job in this crummy motel."

"What legends?" I asked.

"Well, beats me why I should waste my sweet time telling you this, but there's this story about the Lost Dutchman Mine—a fortune in gold, some say, just waiting to be found. There's this rock thing called Weaver's Needle that's supposed to point the way to the mine, if you know when and how to look at it. Maybe it's got a big sign: 'This way to the gold mine' that lights up." With this the man cackled.

"How do I get to this needle?"

"Just follow your nose, west of Route 60, until you come to King's Ranch. Hang a left down a gravel road and you can't miss it." For a moment the man gave me a thoughtful look, then handed over a small thermos. "Here, I'll be danged if I know why I'm doing this, but I reckon you'll be needing this if you're figuring on tramping through the desert."

Thanking the man, I handed him a donut and headed out of town. Even though the legend sounded stupid, there was still something about it that seemed almost possible. Here in this vast open land of strange shapes and mirages anything might be possible. And if this needle could point to some silly Dutchman mine, maybe it could point to other things as well.

After hiking for several hours, I rested and drank from the thermos. Whatever it contained, it was cold and sweet. And, like the bag of donuts, it never ran out. I gazed out over the mountains to the north and there, dead ahead, was Weaver's Needle. It didn't look at all like what I'd imagined. Instead of a needle, it was more like a big rocky fist with its index finger pointing straight up at the sky.

But what could it be pointing at? For a moment I stared up into the blue. But there was only a hawk soaring high above and a small plane pulling a banner that read: "Eat at Geronimo's Deli."

The sign made me hungry, so I sat down on a boulder and ate a donut. Geronimo. What was it about that name? I wondered. Why did it echo so in my head? I looked eastward out over the distant mountains. This was Apache country, I knew. Land of Geronimo, Cochise and potatoes. Potatoes? What made me think of potatoes? Maybe the sun was getting to me.

Then my eye suddenly caught upon a long shadow stretching across the desert floor. It was cast by the needle, in the rays of the setting sun. I jumped up and ran toward the shadow, following its tip eastward as it slowly moved across the ground. It was pointing directly at a tall red cliff, which was rounded in a most peculiar way. Then, as the sun set, the shadow disappeared.

As good a sign as any, I thought, so I began to hike in the direction of the red cliff. All night long I walked. The full moon lit up the desert canyons, revealing pale ghostly shapes. Purplish hoodoo boulders turned into fierce Apache riders on horseback, while the screams of unknown animals became the blood-curdling cries of miners or settlers being scalped. Once, I even stumbled over one of their bodies, though closer inspection revealed it to be merely a dead saguaro cactus. And, growing ever closer, was the red cliff, which was slowly assuming a remarkable profile.

At dawn I had reached the base of the cliff and could finally make out its true form. It was a giant red head, an Indian's head. And from somewhere near the top there came the tapping of hammer and chisel.

"Hello, up there!" I yelled.

"Hello, yourself!" replied the old woman, who was hanging from a rope suspended over the nose of Geronimo. She glanced down at me, then resumed chiseling and cussing at the bare rock. Dressed in a dust-covered smock and sombrero, her long gray hair hung in two long braids down to her waist. "Drat! Hurry up with those explosives!" she yelled. "Take the elevator round back."

"What explosives?" I shouted.

"Why, the explosives I ordered, you nitwit! Aren't you the delivery boy? Get a move on!"

"No, my name is Boggle. All I've got is donuts."

"What do you mean, toggle? I didn't order any toggles. And I don't give a hoot if you think I'm nuts."

"Donuts!" I shouted, cupping my hands. "Donuts for breakfast. Why don't you come on down so we can stop shouting."

"I am not pouting!" said the woman, angrily. "But hold your horses and I'll join you. Might as well have some breakfast. Can't seem to get anything done around here today."

I watched in amazement as the woman pulled herself up the steep cliff and swung up over the top like a gibbon. In no time at all she was down from the cliff face, walking briskly toward me. Her step had the bouncing energy of a little girl. Her face, though, was gnarled and weather-beaten, like the bark of an ancient bristlecone pine.

"They call me Granny Spud," she said, adjusting her hearing aid, "and a lot of other things, besides. Folks say it's because of all the taters I eat. Don't much care what they call me, so long as they leave me alone. What did you say your name was, and what in blazes are you doing way out here?"

"John Boggle's my name, and I'm searching for my lost family."

"Well," she said, scratching her head and rolling a toothpick from one side of her mouth to the other, "haven't seen too many families around here, except for that mixed up carful that made a wrong turn for Disneyland. Boy, were they ever disappointed. But come on, let's talk over breakfast. My campfire's over there."

57

And so, over a breakfast of donuts and baked potatoes, we each told our stories. Granny told me how she had first come to these mountains to be alone after her husband had died. "At least I think he died. To be honest, I can't even remember if I ever had a husband or family. Funny how the mind plays tricks on you. Why, it seems like just yesterday that I first came here, yet I feel like I've been here forever. All I know is, this is where I belong, and where I'll die, God willin'. There's something about the Apaches who lived here that makes my blood rush. I always wanted to come here, to walk the same canyons and mountaintops that Apache feet knew, to breathe the same free air that filled their brave chests."

"Then I discovered this red cliff you see. It used to be called Apache Leap. According to a local story, a small group of Apache warriors were trapped up there by the U.S. Cavalry. With no ammunition left, the Apaches had but one choice. Surrender was just not in their nature. So they jumped off the cliff, yelling 'Geronimo.' Townsfolk in Superior claim they all fell to their deaths on the rocks below. I know different, though. Like a flock of red-tailed hawks, they just flew off westward into the setting sun."

"Well, as soon as I heard that story, a flash went off in my brain. It was as if those braves had been trying to tell me in one word what to do with my life. Geronimo! I would turn this unknown heap of rock into a statue greater than Mount Rushmore, where all who come would be reminded of the glory of Geronimo and the Apache nation. And so here you found me, shaping this rock and my life into something worthwhile. I'm almost finished now. What do you think of him?"

I stared at Granny, then gazed up at the face of red rock. "It's, it's ... bigger than you and me and this whole country. It's beautiful. And so are you."

Granny looked at me, then put her leathery hand upon my head. "Now it's your turn. Tell me, how did you lose your family?"

So I repeated, word for word, my strange story. "Like your monument," I told her, "it is still incomplete. At least you know how your face will turn out. As for me, I can't say where this story will take me or how it will end. All I know is, I must follow it."

"Your story, like that of the Apaches, has a powerful magic. It pulls on me in ways that I can't explain. I feel strangely as if I'm a part of it, though I've never laid eyes on you before."

"You *are* part of it," I said. "I don't know how or why but you are. From the moment I came here, something told me that you're connected to all that I am and once was. Will you join me in my search?"

For a long time, Granny sat in silence. Then, abruptly, she sprang to her feet. "I must go to the top of the cliff to meditate. Remain here, John, until I return."

It wasn't until sunset that she finally came down from the cliff. She was driving a white minivan. It appeared brand new, though some of the paint on the front and rear doors was badly scraped, and in place of a back seat there was a beat up old mattress. "Hop aboard!" she said, opening the door. I picked up my knapsack and got in.

"Something about your story touches my spirit, John Boggle. My work here is almost done, and I feel that in some mysterious way my destiny now lies with you. After lengthy discussion with the spirits of these mountains, they have instructed me to borrow this vehicle and proceed on this journey. Where to, my friend?"

I peered through the windshield and frowned. Which way to go? Each horizon seemed to promise new possibilities. Then I noticed a bright star in the west, shining directly over a distant purple mountain peak. It was the evening star, though some call it the planet Venus. "That way! Follow that star!"

Chapter 12-The Search for Intelligent Life

Driving westward on Route 60, we followed the star as best we could. Though I was pretty sure it wasn't really a star but the planet Venus, it did not act at all like the Venus I knew. Several times, just as it was about to set below the horizon, it would start moving up again in the opposite direction. Retrograde motion, I think it's called, though for the life of me I couldn't remember where I'd heard that. Several times, we almost lost it—once behind the bright skyscrapers of downtown Phoenix, and again in a sandstorm on Route 10, near the Eagle Tail Mountains.

"Do you think it's another sign?" asked Granny. "Or are you just wishing on a star?"

"I don't know. It's not much to go on, but it's all I've got. Do you have any better suggestions?"

"Nope. Just checking" And with that Granny began to whistle as we crossed the California line.

On and on we drove through the land of the Joshua trees, where the lakes are all dry, and through the fabled Palm Springs oasis, where the desert gives way to fountains and green grass. And all the while the evening star glowed before us on the far horizon.

As we followed Route 10 into Los Angeles, however, the star became harder and harder to see as it moved ever closer to the horizon. Finally, we lost it entirely in the City's perpetual dream glow.

"So what do we do now?" asked Granny.

"Look for more signs, I guess. How about that big one on the hill?" We were just about to head toward a sign that read "Hollywood," when I noticed a white, dome-shaped object on a distant hill northeast of Altadena. Fireworks were exploding over it, like brightly colored flowers.

"That looks more promising," I said.

North of the city's outskirts, we soon found ourselves ascending a narrow road that eventually led to a huge mountaintop observatory. In the parking lot was a slight young woman in a white lab coat. Laughing hysterically, she was jumping up and down, setting off fireworks, one right after another.

"I've found you!" she cried at the sky. "You really exist! I never doubted it for one second."

Then she lit another rocket and blew a kiss into space. "To you, my lovelies."

"Found who?" asked Granny.

The woman turned around in surprise. She had not seen the minivan pull up, and didn't recognize the two people standing in front of her. But she was far too happy for worry. "Why, the Venusians, of course! On this very night, after years of careful observation, I have discovered indisputable proof of intelligent life on Venus. No more jokes behind my back. No more lonely nights in the observatory. All the world will know me—Patricia Palomar, discoverer of the Venusians." Then she looked more closely at her visitors.

"Sorry, you must think I'm a real nut case. I've been so absorbed and out of touch with the world up here that I've forgotten my manners. What did you say your names were?"

"I'm John Boggle, and this is Granny Spud. We have followed the sign of the evening star all the way westward from Arizona, until we lost it in the bright horizon of Los Angeles. But then we saw your shining observatory and all the fireworks. We thought it might be another sign."

"A sign of what?" asked Patricia.

"My lost family."

"I see. When did you first notice they were missing?"

"It's a long story. Would you like a donut?"

Patricia gave me, then Granny, a long perplexed look. "Sure, why not? But it's cold out here. Let's go inside the observatory. I've been dying to show somebody my photos."

Inside, Patricia led us to her desk, which was covered with close-up photographs of the planet Venus, taken with the large telescope. "I took these shots last night with a new kind of film. It's sensitive only to a certain wavelength of light—bioviolet, to be exact. Astronomers have been trying to photograph Venus with everything from infrared to ultraviolet, but never with bioviolet. This light is given off by a kind of microscopic sea creature when it's excited. It allows us to see through the surface of things, showing details of the planet never observed before, not even with space probes. But there's more to it than that. We didn't see these details because we don't know how to look or even what we're looking for. All we see is what we expect—a bunch of cracks, craters, and volcanoes." She showed us a photo, with a small area circled in red. "See there? Looks like just another volcano on the planet's surface, right? But my calculations show that the object is actually located many miles *above* the surface, floating within the super dense layer of carbon dioxide that surrounds the whole planet. And if you look closely, you'll see that the object is transparent. Notice the escalator inside? It's an atmospheric shopping mall, I figure. Though I have still not been able to directly observe the Venusians, I propose that they inhabit the higher reaches of the atmosphere where temperatures are less hellish, swimming through their world much like long-finned deep sea creatures do on Earth. Here's another photograph. See that feature that resembles a long fissure lined with small cracks? Well it isn't a fissure at all, but a floating banner, and if you look closer you'll see that the cracks are words:

> WELCOME EARTHLINGS.
> ALL MAJOR CREDIT CARDS
> ACCEPTED.

"See, they must be intelligent! But enough of my story for now. Tell me some more about yourselves. And where on earth did you get these delicious garlic donuts?"

So beneath the slit of open sky in the observatory's great dome, I repeated the story, adding fresh new colors and details. The story was like a painting that grew and grew before us, absorbing us all into its grand silly vision.

When I had finished, Granny added her own special strokes. Then, for awhile, the now dark observatory was deathly quiet, like a funeral parlor.

At last Patricia spoke. "And they call *me* foolish for believing in Venusians! You can't just imagine your family away and then back again. Do you really expect to find them this way?"

"There is no other way," I said. "All I have is this story. I must believe in it, just as you have always believed in the Venusians."

"Yes, but at least I now have proof. What proof do you have that your story is true?"

"There are all kinds of proof," said Granny. "While you take portraits of Venusians in space, John offers us a different kind of portrait—a portrait of a family that might have been or could be. For now I choose to believe in this portrait because I see myself in it. And I must find out why."

"I'll admit, there is something to John's story that rings true. According to the latest research, the brain reacts to an experience by hooking it up with an existing memory in its neurons and then reinforcing the connections between them. These connections are like words, and the brain somehow puts them altogether and stores that experience into a kind of little story called an engram. It is quite possible that all we are is nothing but a bunch of neural connections.

"Are you saying that my family is just an engram?"

"Don't take it personally. Yes, John, but there's more. We also know that engrams tend to follow the "use it or lose it" principle. We mostly remember the things that are important to us and forget those that are not. Everything we are and hope to be is determined by what we bind together from the past. Because you stopped thinking of your family as meaningful anymore, you may have somehow reversed this process of memory storage. By tampering as you did with your memories of them, you not only changed your own reality but destroyed the living engram of your family. The only way to get them back would be to search for connections and somehow reassemble the code that your brain used to store them. Oh, this sounds like mumbo jumbo, but I had a weird feeling the moment the two of you arrived. You're like characters from a book or movie. But how do I fit in?"

"Do you have a family?" asked Granny.

"Of course, I've got a family. Why, there's my ... let me see now, well ... just wait, they're on the tip of my tongue. You know, I've been up here so long that I honestly can't remember them. I can't even remember when I first came here. My life has just been one big lonely search. And now that I've found what I've been looking for, it all seems so pointless without a family to share it with."

"There's your answer," I told her. "Come join us."

"Well, I suppose the Venusians can wait a little while longer before being introduced to the world. I need a vacation anyway. And I'm just dying to find out how this story of yours turns out. Just give me a minute to lock up."

So we piled into the minivan and drove back down the winding mountain road. "Where to?" asked Granny.

"I'm fresh out of signs right now," I said. "Why don't we just head back to Route 10 and keep going westward as long as we can."

In a short while, however, Route 10 ended abruptly in Santa Monica. There was only one way westward, and that was Route 1, the Pacific Coast Highway. We followed it past Santa Barbara until it began heading northwestward to Morro Bay and the windswept cliffs of Monterey. But though the way was filled with postcard images and signs for every kind of tourist attraction, not one of them offered what we were looking for.

"Has anyone noticed we're now heading north?" asked Patricia. "I thought we were going to keep heading west?"

"Way I figure it, we have two choices," said Granny, pulling off the highway into a scenic rest area. "Ditch the minivan and rent a boat to go west, or stay on this road until something turns up. At least we've got wheels. I say we keep driving north or wherever the signs lead us."

"All right, but we still need some motivation," said Patricia. "John, wake up. We need another sign."

I rubbed my eyes and looked out over the vast blue Pacific Ocean. There were tankers and sailboats and a small pod of migrating gray whales. And the usual oil slicks, gulls, and floating garbage. In the parking lot, overflowing trash cans had become mountains of wrappers, bottles, and cans. My eyes followed a stream of litter that seemed to point back to the highway. "That's it! Follow the trash road!"

The others stared at me as if I'd finally lost my marbles. "How can we follow trash?" asked Patricia.

"I'm not exactly sure," I said, beginning to doubt my gut feeling. Then I noticed a sign for Trashville, Oregon-700 miles. "There's our answer!"

Chapter 13-A Future in Trash

So, filled with new hope, we drove north on Route 1 until it merged with 101. Munching on donuts and singing songs of the open road, we passed through the Great Redwood Forest and on into Oregon. We could tell we were getting closer to Trashville by how clean the highway was and by all the green-and-white signs (made from scrap wood yet very attractive) which read "Trash is Us; Top Dollars for Trash; City of Tomorrow."

Just north of Tillamook, we caught our first sight of the city on the horizon—a city like none we had ever seen. Its brilliant skyscrapers, constructed out of billions and billions of glass bottles and aluminum cans that each reflected the setting sun, dazzled our eyes, causing Granny to almost drive off the road.

When our eyes finally adjusted, we observed other equally remarkable buildings. Giant domes made out of plastic milk jugs.

Graceful black temples made from columns of old steel-belted tires. Sturdy warehouses made of crushed autos and washing machines. Apartment complexes constructed out of eggshell cartons and bubble gum concrete. Graceful homes with papier-mâché siding and cellophane windows. And running through the very center of the city, spanning the Wilson River, was a bridge composed entirely of wire coat hangers.

"Look at that building over there," I said. "It's like a castle in the sky! Why, it must be a mile high. Let's check it out."

We drove across the bridge toward the huge red building, which we soon noticed was made from endless columns of rusty steel drums. A large sign in front, made of ketchup bottle caps and old sneakers, announced that it was the headquarters of the 4R Company—Resource Recovery, Redemption and Restoration, Inc.—whose motto was "Better Living From Trash."

Parking the minivan in the visitor's lot, we passed through an arched gateway of plastic forks and spoons into a great Styrofoam hall. A guard, dressed in a mishmash of discarded but neatly restored clothes, was sitting at the reception desk. "Who are you looking for?" he asked.

"My family," I said. "Are there any employees here named Boggle?"

"Sorry, no one here with that name."

"Well, could you tell me who's in charge here?"

"Why sure, that would be the company president, Ms. Tina Trashmore. She's on the top floor, Room 5001. But I think she's in a meeting right now."

"That's all right. We'll just go up and wait." I motioned to Granny and Patricia, who were poring over an exhibit of how toxic wastes can be turned into food, and the three of us filed into a luxurious elevator. Its rich paneling looked like mahogany, but it was only laminated Popsicle sticks.

After a long trip to the top floor, we got out and went over to the big observation windows of reinforced cellophane. But all we could see from this height were clouds.

Walking down the hallway, we heard a voice coming from an open door. We peered in, and there at a podium was a short, sturdy woman, with hair tied up in a bun, addressing a crowded auditorium. Though most of her audience was dressed in expensive-looking suits and dresses, she herself was outfitted in an odd but tasteful assortment of secondhand clothes. She smiled at me as we came in and sat down.

On the screen was the title of her talk: "From Landfills to Skyfills ... or Trash Today, Towers Tomorrow." Then, with slides illustrating the latest trash technologies, she lectured the group for a full hour. She spoke with authority and big fancy words, sprinkled with charm and earthy humor.

At the conclusion of her talk, we walked up to the stage and introduced ourselves. "Does the name John Boggle mean anything to you?" I asked.

"Why no," said Tina. "Should it? Come to think of it, there *is* something familiar about you. Didn't I see you at the New York Garbage Festival?"

"I don't think so," I said. "You see, we're searching for my lost family. I just know there's a trash connection somewhere. We simply followed the signs for Trashville and here we are. Would you like a donut?"

"Don't mind if I do. Say, why don't we go into my office for some coffee, and we'll talk some more. And where did you ever get such rugged, tasty donuts?" Tina held one up to the light and tried to bend it. "Good tensile strength. Why, I could build a whole city from these."

"Did you and your company build this entire city?" asked Patricia. "I've never seen anything like it, not even on Venus."

"Let's just say, I had a big hand in it. No real trick to it. You just have to know your materials and what you wish to accomplish with them. And it helps to be a little crazy, because things don't always go exactly the way you planned. The rest is just common sense, hard work, and lots of love. Of course, it also doesn't hurt to be a good scrounger."

They entered a large room that was more like a dump than an office. It was a tidy dump, however. Various materials were arranged in labeled dumpsters, while metal shelves were stacked with file boxes containing every imaginable kind of waste material. On her desk were three broken television sets, a dozen Hula hoops, an old rusty trash can, 27 plastic yogurt cups, and hundreds of old phonograph records. "These are my latest projects. I'm sure there must be a good use for them. Make yourselves at home, please. Now tell me about this lost family."

Sitting on a couch made from a stripped auto seat, I retold the story, which seemed to come easier this time. The words seemed to pour out with a life of their own, surrounding us with strange images. Then Granny and Patricia added some more details, which jumped into their heads in a way they could not explain.

By the time the story had reached its present moment, Tina was in tears. "Oh, it's so sad," she sobbed. "You all seem so alone, I just want to take and hug you." Then she straightened up in her chair and gave a nervous cough. "Of course, that wouldn't be proper, for I've never met you before. At least I don't think so. Listen, I've got a busy schedule and ..."

"Too busy to find a family?" I asked.

"Whatever do you mean? My family's right here." She handed me a framed picture holder that was sitting on a corner of her desk. "See? There they are."

I stared at the three photos. The price tag was still on the glass. "But these are only pictures of movie stars. What about your real family?"

"Silly me. I keep meaning to put them in, it's just that ... well, I've got so many things to do. You know how it is."

"Yes, we all do," said Granny. "Do you mind telling us about this supposed family of yours?"

"I resent that remark! Why, my family is just as real as you are. Just give me a moment. I'm sure I can come up with them. Let's see now, there's ..."

"Oh, give it up, will you?" snapped Patricia, with a wave of her hands. "Can't you see? Despite all your accomplishments, you're still as alone as we are. And the way that you responded to John's, that is, to *our* story, proves you're one of us. Admit it, Tina, you're hooked."

"Well, I suppose it wouldn't hurt if I joined you for awhile. *Somebody* has to look out for you. Mind you, I'm not saying I buy all this. Recovering a lost family isn't easy. It's just that—oh, this sounds so absurd—but even though we just met, I can't bear the thought of your leaving me now. Couldn't we just stay here and live together for a bit?"

I'm afraid not," I said, for we still don't have the whole story. All we know is that we're connected in some way. But we still don't know how or why. We need to find more answers."

"John, do you think we might be some kind of long lost relatives?" asked Granny. "We do seem quite attached for people who have just bumped into each other. Is it possible that when the story finally ends, we'll all live happily ever after?"

"I wish I knew. But I do agree with Tina. Now that we're together, I just can't let you go."

"Well, what are we waiting for?" said Granny. "The trail's getting cold, and we've still got a story to finish. Let's get a move on."

Chapter 14-Doctor Zither and Company

As the moon rose over Trashville, we climbed into the minivan and headed north on Route 101 into Washington, then east and south, all around the Olympic Mountains. The scenery was nice but we really didn't know where we were going, for I was fresh out of signs.

So we roamed through Idaho and Montana, then zigzagged back and forth across the Rocky Mountains all the way south to New Mexico. We drove east for a while. Then we turned around in Texas and rambled north across the Great Plains to the Badlands of South Dakota. We must have visited hundreds of national parks and monuments, each chock-full of bigger than life things. There were geysers, flaming gorges, and sawtoothed mountains. Rainbow bridges, wind caves, and even craters of the moon. There were herds of buffalo, elk, and pronghorns. And once, we almost lost Granny to a grizzly that was trying to take our donuts. But, grand as all these sights were, none led us to our family.

It was 3 a.m. and pitch black, deep within the Dakota Badlands. We had taken a wrong turn onto a nameless back road and were looking for the highway. Everyone was exhausted, but we were too depressed to sleep. For our story, we all realized, was going nowhere.

"This whole thing is beginning to seem pretty weird," said Patricia. "Here we are, the four of us, shooting around like a bunch of silly neutrinos, all because of some stupid story. Maybe we're just trying too hard. Why don't we just relax and enjoy each other's company for awhile? How about a little traveling music?" She turned on the radio and scanned the stations. "Speaking of weird, listen to this."

A strange sad music filled the van. Then a voice began to bellow, as if from the bottom of nothing, a blues song about a man without a family. It was accompanied by the melancholy strains of accordion and zither music, and by a chorus who wailed the blues with a curious assortment of hisses, growls, and screams. "My family done left me," sang the voice.

"That voice, that song!" I shouted. "Where is it coming from?"

"It's from a station in Chicago, I believe," said Patricia. "Sometimes I'll pick it up even in California."

I strained to hear the rest of the lyrics over the static. "We've been so busy *looking* for signs that we've forgotten to listen for them. Follow that song!"

At last we managed to find the highway and so, singing the blues, followed Route 90 all the way to Chicago

"I'm getting pretty tired of sleeping in this van all the time," said Tina, as we drove into the city the following night. "Let's put up in a hotel for a change. I'm buying."

We stopped at the first place we came to, the Best Family Inn, on South Michigan Avenue near Grant Park. And though we had to share the same king-size bed, and though Granny's snores could be heard three floors up, we slept soundly all through the next day till almost midnight.

"Time to do some exploring," I said, shaking Granny, who was still fast asleep with all the blankets wrapped around her. We ate a quick supper of donuts, then hit the streets.

For hours we ambled in silence, down one side street after another, listening to the sounds of the city. We strained our ears for that strange music we had heard on the radio. Almost ready to give up for the night, at last we came to a blues club with a neon sign that read "Buddy Guy's Legends." Appearing tonight only, announced a small sign in the window, was the legendary blues guitarist Buddy Guy himself, along with Eric Clapton, Lefty Dizz, and the incomparable Doctor Zither and his Blue Moon Menagerie. Perhaps it was only the weird name of the last group, but something about it struck a chord, so we went in.

We sat down at a table in the back corner and ordered drinks. "I'll have a beer," I told the waiter. "It's my story and I can do whatever I want."

"You'll have a soda," said Tina in a stern voice. "It's my story, too."

For the next two hours we listened and swayed, as Buddy Guy, Eric Clapton, and mean Lefty Dizz made the kind of music that turned the soul inside out. But the most awesome group was yet to come.

At 2 a.m. a tall monster of a man appeared on the stage. He was dressed in a gorilla suit, with a black fedora and dark sunglasses. As he began to snuffle and strum his electric bass zither, the crowd roared. "Yo, Doctor! Doctor Zither!"

He put down his zither and took up his accordion. Then, one by one, the other members of the band made their appearance. There was an emu, a wallaby, and a fat capybara. Followed by a Tasmanian devil, a shapely okapi, and a Komodo dragon. And three six-foot cockroaches in blue spandex suits. (The other animals wore only the costumes that nature gave them.)

"I'm gonna tell you a story," wailed Doctor Zither, as the others crooned and played in the background, "of a poor man who's got no family."

Everyone in the place was tapping their feet and swinging to the music, especially a little white-haired woman, in a black suit and hat, who was sitting in front. "You tell 'em, Doc!" she yelled, suddenly jumping up on the table and dancing. "Let it all hang out!"

All during his performance, however, Doctor Zither kept staring at us as if we were far more legendary than anyone else in the club. When he was through playing his last encore, he took off his gorilla suit and came over to our table. "Who *are* you guys?" he asked.

"Boggle's the name, Doctor," I said, slapping him a high five, "and family's our game. Won't you sit down and join us?"

"Sure enough," said Doc. "Say, Joe," he yelled over to the bartender. "Mix me one of my specials, will ya? I figure I'm going to need it. Now tell me more, Mr. Boggle, about this game of yours."

As a waiter brought over a bubbling drink, filled with purple bananas and little pink things swimming about, the white-haired woman walked over and plunked herself down. Beneath her black suit jacket she wore a white

81

Doctor Zithers T-shirt and a gold pendant of a cockroach guitarist. "Hey, wait for Soul Lady! I want to hear this tune, too."

So I told him my version of the family blues, while the others backed me up with their own solos.

"Man, this is some weird trip you're all on," said Doc, but, then, I like it weird. There's something about you guys. We all seem to be singing the same song. Mind if I tag along for awhile? I could use some new material for my gig."

"Sure, but what about the rest of your band?" I asked.

"Oh, don't worry about them. Most of them want to go solo, anyway. It's tough keeping a good band together. Why don't you guys come over to my apartment and we'll rap some more. And say, could I have another one of those donuts?"

"Wait for me!" said Soul Lady. "I'm in this gig, too."

We went over to Doc's apartment, which was just above a pet store in the West End, and talked until almost dawn, replaying the story from every angle. But in the wee hours of the morning, we began to have our doubts. It was a great story so far, we all agreed, but maybe it was just that and no more. And maybe we were just six lonely people who got along so well simply because we had nothing else to believe in.

Suddenly, there was a hard knock at the door. Cautiously, Doc opened it, and there stood a hulking bear of a policeman, who looked as if he were just out of hibernation. "Who's the driver of that minivan?" he growled.

"I am!" shouted Granny. "What of it?"

"You're under arrest for theft of a U.S. Postal vehicle. You have the right to ..."

"Hold everything!" I said. "Granny, did you steal that van?"

"Land sakes, no! I only borrowed it for a time. Why are they making a federal case out of this?"

The policeman put handcuffs on Granny and began leading her away. "We're all in this together," I said. "If she goes, we go." Then we all blocked the doorway.

"Suit yourselves," said the policeman. "You're all under arrest for interfering with the duties of a police officer ... Ow!" Soul Lady was crouched on her knees, with her mouth firmly attached to his leg. "And for biting him!" Then he cuffed us and led us all down to the station.

There we were booked and taken down endless stone steps to a dark, wet basement. All the other cells were full that morning, with an assortment of murderers, armed robbers, and jaywalkers. Some of them jeered as the six of us filed past their doors to our small windowless cell.

As the steel door locked behind us, there came a snorting and snickering from the farthest dark corner. And then a foul, nasal voice. "So glad you dropped in."

Chapter 15-Imprisoned with an Impostor

Doc held up his lighter. In the shadows, sitting on the toilet, was a squat, hunched up figure. He was draped with a dirty blanket, with only his big bulbous nose showing. It glowed like a purple mushroom in the dim light.

"It's about time they sent me some company," said the figure. "Have a seat."

At the sound of that voice I grimaced. It grated on my nerves like a bad song played backward. Yet something about it seemed awfully familiar.

"Who are you?" I asked, peering at the purple nose.

"Oh, why not just call me Jake—Jake the Fake. Everybody else does. I've had more different names and identities than I can recall." He scratched himself under the blanket. "I've been just about everything you can think of—jet pilot, priest, podiatrist, even an uncle, once. I was doing all right, too, fooling everybody, until one day I tried being a president—President of the United States, that is. Got caught trying to sell off California and, well, here I am. By the way, can any of you gals sew? My pants need mending." He picked up a pair of greasy, grimy pants off the floor and threw them straight at Patricia.

"Yuck! Why, of all the nerve!" She hurled the pants back at the corner. "John, who *is* this guy? Is he part of the story?"

"I'm afraid he is, though how or why I can't say. Just looking at him makes me want to throw up. He's like a bad amusement park ride, which makes you sick not once but every time you think of it."

"Look, Jake, or whoever you are," said Patricia. "I don't do pants and I don't like you! And if you think I'm going to put up with ..."

"How come I always get stuck with losers?" said Jake. "What's the matter with women today? Why can't they do pants?" Then he snorted. "In some ways you remind me of some folks I once lived with. Don't remember too much about them, except that they all seemed headed for nowhere."

"Who are you calling a loser?" said Doc. He strutted over to Jake and was about to say something in his face, when a big hairy arm shot out of the blanket and grabbed him by the leg. Doc bellowed as he was spun and thrown across the room.

"You monster!" cried Soul Lady, beating on Jake's nose. "How dare you pick on Doctor Zither?"

Again the hairy arm shot out. Soul Lady flitted across the room like a bug. "Come on, who's next?" said Jake.

"John, say something!" said Granny. "Is this some sort of sign or what?"

"I'm not sure. Part of it seems to fit, and part of it doesn't. It's all so confusing. I just don't know."

"I'll tell you what it is," said Patricia. "It's a sign we're all losing it. I mean, look at us. We've been locked up with a crazy woman who goes around stealing postal vehicles. And now we're being pushed around by some big nose thing over there, while John, our fearless leader, has suddenly lost his way. Maybe we *are* losers."

"Nobody forced you to tag along," shouted Granny. "And, as for being crazy, Ms. Venus Lady ..."

"Oh, yeah? Well, take that, you old windbag!" She threw a donut at Granny, which hit Doc instead.

"Hey, watch it!" he said. Then he picked up a pillow and started whacking Patricia and Granny, while Soul Lady started biting everyone.

"Stop it, stop it!" shouted Tina. "This is no way for a family to act. Then, again, maybe it is, who knows?" She walked calmly over to Jake and put her arms around him.

"Let me go! Let me go!" he screamed. Arms thrashing, he struggled furiously, but there was no getting away from Tina's iron grip.

"He's an ugly cuss, all right," said Tina. "He seems to bring out the very worst in all of us. But I feel that he has a role to play in our family story, and even if it's a fake role, we must take him along. There's a good use for everything and everyone, I say. Maybe we can salvage this character yet. What do you say to that, Jake?"

"I say you're full of garbage! Let me up!"

"Here, put on your pants," said Tina, "and if you give me any more lip, I'll wrap you up in that blanket and carry you."

"OK, so we take Jake with us," said Patricia. "But we still have to find a way out of here." At this Jake snickered again. Then he sat up quickly as if to hide something behind the toilet.

"I think you know something," said Tina.

"Fools! Even if I did, do you think I'd tell you? You're stuck with me. We're just one big happy family now."

In one calm, quick motion, Tina yanked one of Jake's arms behind his back and slammed him against the wall. "You were saying?"

"Uncle, uncle!" he cried. "You're breaking my arm! Let up and I'll tell you."

"Not till you sing for us, Jake."

"OK, there's an old sewer line that runs along the back of this cell. For months I've been using this rusty spoon to scrape the mortar away from the bricks near the toilet. Some of them are almost loose."

Releasing Jake, Tina went over to the wall. She pushed on one of the bricks until it slid out and dropped with a splash behind the wall. Immediately, a wet rotten smell poured out of the hole and filled the cell. It was enough to make even Tina almost faint.

"Come on!" she said, staggering from the fumes. "Help me with these bricks." And in a short time they had cleared a hole large enough for them to pass into the sewer tunnel.

Doc held out his lighter and poked his head through the hole. The tunnel was about eight feet high. In both directions the floor was covered with dark pools of water. "Only one problem, fellow soul mates. Which way do we go? I've been down before, but I sure don't want to end up at the bottom of some sewage treatment plant."

"There are worse things than sewage," I said, looking at Jake. Then, grabbing my knapsack, I plunged through the smelly dark hole.

Chapter 16-A Remembrance of Things Smelled

As usual, I didn't know where I was going. I just knew I had to get away from that scene and start moving toward something—anything—even if it was just a smell. From far behind me I could hear Soul Lady shouting, "Wait for us!" But I couldn't stop. Like the notes of some strange smelly music from another world, that horrible scent of sewage pounded in my brain, hurling me down the tunnel toward its source. But as I ran I couldn't help wondering. How can you smell music? And why was it so familiar?

On and on I went in the pitch blackness, sloshing through ankle-deep waters, with only my nose to guide me. A couple of times I stumbled and fell. Pushing myself up from the water, I shuddered once as something slimy wriggled under my hand.

Soon I had lost all track of time and space. From the feel of the walls I could tell that the tunnel had forked a number of times, with countless side branches. Like a rat in a dark maze, I tried to follow the smell in whatever direction it seemed strongest, but there was really little difference to go on. The smell was all around me now, so much so that it seemed to have become a part of me. And for some crazy reason it made me smile and almost feel at home.

I stopped running and turned around to listen. Then I cupped my hands and yelled. "Anybody out there?" But there was no sound of the others. There was only a steady drip, drip, drip ... and a faint sloshing, like something dragging itself through the water.

To go back now and try to find them in that dark tunnel would be foolhardy, I told myself. They could have taken any one of dozens of different forks and side passages. But I had no great faith in going forward, either, or in even knowing what forward meant anymore. So I squatted down and took a long swig from the thermos. The liquid was cool and sweet, like lemonade, this time. Then I ate two donuts, which tasted just like cheeseburgers. "If I ever get out of here," I promised myself, "I'll make a million on these."

With a warm glow in my stomach at least, I decided to just keep on moving, trusting my faithful nose to find a new sign. For what seemed like eons I plodded and sniffed, occasionally laughing out loud at my absurd predicament. Then from somewhere above my head there came a distant rumbling like thunder. Now what?

I forgot the sound, however, as I came to yet another fork in the tunnel. From the right I could feel an ever so slight breeze blowing softly on my face. Though it still smelled like sewage, there was a faint trace of other smells mixed in—a subtle blend of exhaust fumes, dog doodle, cheap perfume, rotting fruit and coffee grounds ... and garlic! All of a sudden I felt myself wishing for a heavy duty nose, one that could really deliver the goods.

I sniffed and I sniffed till my nose went raw. The smells called up images, strange images that I could not explain. And they reminded me of that dead house in South Providence, only it wasn't dead anymore. It was filled with a family, a truly weird family that...

I felt dizzy from all the crazy pictures spinning around in my head. The worst one of all was the ugly face of Jake the Fake. Why was I so afraid of it? And could someone that awful really be part of our family? Suddenly I remembered how he once gripped my shoulder with his vise-like hand and dared me to get up from my chair. The smell of stale beer and cabbage on his breath made me want to puke. No matter how hard I struggled, I couldn't get away from him. He just laughed as if it were a big joke. I started to cry and he called me a big sissy and other things. Told me I'd never be a man. I hated him for making me so afraid.

But there was something else—what was it? Then I remembered. How one night that horrible face suddenly appeared over my bed and I felt my hand being pulled down into the darkness to touch … No! It didn't really happen. I must have imagined it.

Shaking with shame and anger, I threw up till there was nothing left inside me. I leaned my hand weakly against what I thought was the wall, but instead found myself falling into one of the side tunnels. Clutching blindly for something to hold on to, I managed to grab a soft, bulbous thing.

"Ouch! Something's got my nose!" came the nasal voice. Then a small light flashed in my eyes.

"Hey, everybody! It's John!" shouted Doc.

For a while we were like some multi-armed cave creature, with arms waving and squeezing each other in the darkness, all except those of Jake. His nose still throbbing, he was hopping around like a mad toad, cussing at me. But I was much too happy to notice.

"Oh, settle down," said Tina, pulling on Jake's suspenders. "We thought we'd lost you, for sure, John. And our ugly friend here wasn't much help. I think he even tried to get us more lost than we already were. I'm beginning to wonder if it wasn't a mistake in taking him."

"He's one big mistake, if you ask me," said Granny, with an icy stare. "I just can't imagine him ever being a part of our family tree. Story or no story, I say we dump Mr. Jake the Fake right here."

Suddenly there was a loud rumbling from up above. And from somewhere far down the tunnel came a violent roar. "What in heaven's name is that?" said Soul Lady.

"If it's what I think it is," said Tina, "then we're about to become a drowned family. That rumbling you heard was thunder, which means rain. And since most likely this is a storm sewer, I foresee us all embarking on a rather abrupt journey to wherever Chicago's runoff takes us. Quick, everybody, grab whatever pieces of solid trash you can see or put your hands on. It doesn't have to be pretty—just make sure it floats. "

"What good will that do?" shouted Patricia.

"No time to explain. Just do it!" said Tina. "And give me all your belts and shoelaces!"

Too frightened to argue, we all did as we were told, all except Jake. "I'm through taking orders from you or the rest of this crazy bunch!" With arms folded, he just stood there scowling.

I walked over and put my nose right up to his. It still made me sick to look at him.

But no longer did he appear frightening—just a scowling, scared brat. "Then we'll just leave you here all by yourself." Then, turning around, I stumbled off into the darkness to look for scrap.

Grumbling, Jake unlaced his dirty, high top sneakers. "No need to get all huffy, John. Can't you take a joke?"

In a few minutes, the group had assembled a large pile of assorted trash. There were weathered pieces of wood, old doors and crates, plastic bottles, as well as many things that none of us could identify, but at least they floated. Then, using the belts and shoelaces along with the plastic from hundreds of six-pack holders, Tina's hands began moving like a whirlwind, and in very short order she had constructed a small, sturdy craft. "Get inside, everyone! Hurry!"

As the last member of our party climbed into the boat, it was picked up like a peanut shell by the rising foamy waters and went hurtling down the tunnel.

Chapter 17-Voyage of the Boggle Queen

Lying facedown, we held on for dear life as our little trash boat rode the crest of the storm surge. On and on we went, caught in a never-ending nightmare, through the darkness beneath the city. The craft shook so hard at times that it seemed to be breaking up. Finally, we just shot out of a drainpipe, straight into the South Branch of the Chicago River. From there we were carried swiftly into the Chicago Sanitary Canal.

As the storm clouds parted, our crew peeked over the stern at the quickly receding skyline, then held our breath again as two barges narrowly missed our boat on either side.

"Hey, anybody know where we're going?" asked Doc.

"Feels like southwest," said Granny, with eyes closed and face turned toward the morning sun. "That's always a good direction. Any signs on the horizon, John?"

"No," I answered, dreamily. "And I'm too tired to even think right now. Maybe we should just drift awhile and see where the current takes us. There are worse things than drifting."

"Not a bad idea," said Tina. "We've all been through quite a wringer. A nice cruise might help us unwind. Maybe it'll even help us remember. But, first, we need a name for our proud vessel. I propose we call her The Boggle Queen. What do you think, John?"

"Sounds good to me. But let's give her a proper ceremony."

We landed on a little spit near Joliet, where the canal joined the Illinois River. "I christen thee The Boggle Queen," I announced in my most solemn voice, pouring liquid from the thermos over the nose of our boat. Then, after a brief lunch of donuts, we shoved off again into the river.

Now westward we drifted, through the great Gebhard Woods, past Buffalo Rock and on into Spring Valley. Then southwestward again to Peoria, Chautauga, and Meredosia. For many carefree days we traveled, as if in a dream. It was a peaceful landscape, dotted with blue lakes and small towns, where a family might stay safely hidden forever from the storms of this world. The weather was clear and warm, with not a dark cloud in sight. Even Jake had stopped complaining for a time.

Then, one day, at a bend in the river near Grafton, we watched in quiet wonder as our craft slowly drifted out into the broad arms of the Mississippi, Father of Waters.

It was near St. Louis, Missouri, that we finally decided to put up for a few days and find some temporary work. It seemed like the thing to do. For, despite how close we were beginning to feel toward each other (excluding Jake, of course) and no matter how hard we tried, we still couldn't remember just how our old family was put together. And we knew that our journey had to end and soon. Maybe by working at various odd jobs, we thought, we could find some clues that would tell us who we were.

While Doc sang at the zoo for quarters and dimes, Patricia washed dishes and recited poetry at a vegetarian restaurant on Market Street. Tina made craft items out of trash, which she sold to tourists in Mullanphy Square; she also kept an eye on Jake, who just sat in the park, feeding pigeons. Granny and Soul Lady both volunteered at a soup kitchen on Martin Luther King Boulevard.

I too looked for work, but try as I might, I just couldn't seem to find the right job. So I stayed behind at our campground on the river, guarding our boat and scanning the want ads for some kind of sign.

Though our job experiences did help to stir up memories, they were still as murky as the Mississippi and gave us no real clues. So we took a vote and decided to shove off again and just go with the flow, as far as the river might take us.

Down to Memphis, Tennessee, we drifted and twisted, around Ox Bend and Helena, Arkansas, and over to Lake Providence, Louisiana. There we stopped for a while, fishing for clues in its placid blue waters, but all we got was a dead catfish.

It was while floating through Baton Rouge and on into New Orleans that we all began to worry as one, for no river runs forever. What would we do when the river ended?

We did not have long to fret. South of New Orleans, our river highway suddenly branched into channels, which fanned out into a broad delta and faded into the Gulf of Mexico.

East of Tidewater, our party put ashore to get some bearings. As we climbed out, Jake somehow managed to get himself stuck in a sandbar.

"Help!" he screamed. "Don't leave me!" But the more he struggled, the further he sunk. Already up to his waist, he was whimpering like a lost puppy.

I confess that for a few seconds I savored the sight of him sinking further and further up to his neck and then his nose. Then I jumped into action. It took all of our combined efforts, but finally we managed to pull him out. Caked with muck and exhausted, we dragged ourselves up to higher ground and rested for what couldn't have been more than an hour. It was only then that we remembered the boat, but it was too late. We stood on the shore, watching helplessly as our craft along with my knapsack slowly drifted out and then vanished into the sea horizon.

"It's a good thing I kept this dead catfish," said Doc, pulling it out of his pocket.

Chapter 18-Travels of a Mixed Up Man

"Well, John, any suggestions?" asked Granny.

"I guess we just head back to Tidewater. It's either that or swim."

"Brilliant!" said Patricia. "Our great leader has spoken. Where would we be without him?"

So, with weary hearts, we trudged back across the delta. When we came to the Great River Road we decided, after a quick discussion, to follow it north to New Orleans. There was really little choice, since it was the only road in town.

All night long we walked without so much as a word. Even Jake was strangely quiet. With blanket drawn up over his head, he looked like a muddy monk in contemplation. The damp warm air felt heavy in our chests. From the swamps came the incessant roar of pig frogs and, occasionally, the bellowing of a bull alligator. "Reminds me of my band," said Doc. Though we were all exhausted, no one dared to lie down and sleep. And no one had the slightest idea of what we would do in New Orleans. But on everyone's mind was the same unspeakable thought. Maybe it was finally time for us to split up and go our separate ways, just as the river had done.

Only a few cars had passed us all night, and none had offered a ride. Then, just past Happy Jack, a beat-up pickup truck slowed down and stopped. A bearded man in a fishhook-studded Panama hat poked his head out the window. "Bon soir, mes amis. Climb aboard."

A Cajun fisherman, he was bringing his nightly catch into New Orleans. We all clambered into the truck bed, making ourselves as comfortable as we could among the ice-covered fish.

At dawn the truck stopped in front of a seafood restaurant in the French Quarter. The smell of fresh beignets filled the air, reminding us of the lost donuts and how hungry we were. Thanking the fisherman, we followed the aroma to a little cafe on Decatur Street.

There, in a corner booth, over gallons of cafe au lait and dozens of sweet beignets, we tried our best to brace ourselves for whatever future awaited us. "Guess I'm all out of signs,"

I confessed. "I just don't know how to finish our story."

"Oh, don't look so glum," said Patricia. "It's not so bad. We've still got each other, and we can always find work."

"That's right," said Tina. "So we don't remember who we are. Big deal. We'll just start a new story."

"But you don't understand," I said. "We have to finish *this* story. It's the very reason we managed to find each other and the meaning of our life together. Everything we are and hope to be, our past and our future, lies at the end of this story. We're almost there, I can feel it! We just need more time."

"OK, but first things first," said Tina. "We need jobs and a place to stay. Let's hit the streets."

As we wandered up Decatur Street, looking for Help Wanted signs, we happened to pass a little place called The Mexican Dragon Bookshop. I stopped and stared at an announcement in the window. It was for a new book, entitled *Travels of a Mixed up Man*. Below it was a picture of the author.

"What are we stoppin' here for?" asked Doc. "We don't need any books.

But I had already gone inside. The bookshop was crowded with people, excitedly waiting in line. Behind a table stacked high with books sat a middle-aged man with a handlebar mustache and ponytail. Using his pen name,

"Lot O. Jobs," he was busy signing books for his many fans. He thanked each of them personally in a soft, gentle voice that made me shiver. I grabbed one of the books and flipped through the pages. It was all about different jobs the author had held, hundreds of them. Then I turned to the dedication page. It read, "To John and my lost family, wherever you may be."

Shoving past the others, I slammed the book down in front of the author.

"I'm sorry," he said, "but you'll just have to wait in line."

"There's no time for that! Please!"

The man looked at me with a puzzled expression. For a few long moments he said nothing. Then a small smile crept across his face. "All right," he said. "You must be quite a reader. How would you like me to inscribe this?"

My eyes blurred with tears. I tried to speak but I couldn't make the words come out. Then, from deep inside me, the words slowly rose to the surface, liked trapped bubbles of sweet sewer air. "To John," I said ... "with love from Dad."

Chapter 19-A Family Party

Suddenly I was back in my writing room, the old one in South Providence. Gone was my fancy typewriter. And in my hands was a new journal, inscribed to me by my stepfather—no, make that my Dad—along with a suggestion "to go write the story of our family."

Then from the stairs I heard Mom calling. "John, are you up there? Dinner's ready. Everyone's here."

I rushed downstairs to the dining room. This time, it was relatively clean for a change, though a few coat hangers were still scattered about. And there before me was my old family, all dressed up as if for a wedding. Even Bruno had a brand new suit (no gorilla, this time). And Venus, of course, had on her best white robe. Everything was exactly as it was ... with one exception. There was no Uncle Vinnie.

"John, "I'd like you to meet your Aunt Lavinnia," said Mom. "She's from Lithuania."

Smiling, she shook my hand. "I've heard some good things about you," she said in a pleasant voice. She was short and burly, with a rather large nose, but on her it looked perfect. I especially liked the way she didn't try to hug me right off the way some pushy relatives do.

I was about to ask Mom about Uncle Vinnie, then decided not. There was something about Aunt Lavinnia, something that reminded me a little of...

Well, I guess every family can use a little editing.

Chapter 20-The Story of Our Family

It's been three months now since our little adventure to nowhere and back. I've put this off long enough. Guess it's time to get on with the story.

Wish I could say that things have changed a lot, but they haven't. At least "Uncle" Vinnie is gone—good riddance! Or is he? There is something strange about how Aunt Lavinnia suddenly appeared in his absence and how she's got some of the same outward features. Did I just make her up the same way I made up that other family? And if I did, isn't that what got me into trouble the first time? All I know is, Aunt Lavinnia seems real enough and as a person she's nothing at all like Vinnie. She's kind, gentle and intelligent. She's been telling me stories about wizards, castles and knights of old Lithuania. She even helps me with my writing by listening to my stories and patiently going over what she likes and dislikes about each. I can joke around with her, but she keeps things private between us and knows how to keep out of my space. And even though she's got a wicked sense of humor, she's not at all crazy like the rest of my family. I'm glad she's here. Maybe for every vile person in the world there's someone like her to balance things out. At least that's my belief and I'm sticking to it.

Only trouble is, every once in a while when I look at her big nose I get this awful flash of Vinnie. I try to pretend as if nothing's wrong, but it's hard to keep stuff from Aunt Lavinnia. She just looks at me sadly with those deep blue eyes of hers. I don't think I'll ever be rid of Vinnie. Every night I see him, smell him and … Damn him all to hell! But that's another story, one that I'm going to have to live with.

As for the rest of my family, they're all still crazy as ever. But I think I'm finally beginning to understand what makes them tick. I guess I'll start with Dad—the one who's here—the only one that counts. Wish I could say that his book sold a million copies and is at the top of the bestsellers list. And that he's famous and travelling all over the world doing book signings. Yes, he really did publish his book. But he had it printed himself. He says he got a good deal on it, but the pages are made of cheap paper and tend to fall apart if you even stare at the book cross-eyed. Never lacking in self-confidence, he had 10,000 printed, which sent Mom through the roof when she finally found out.

"Sales are a little slow, right now," he tells people. "But I put up a few signs in the neighborhood and I'm thinking of having a book signing party. And I've sent press releases to all the TV stations." Dad still has 9,978 copies left to go.

Meanwhile, Dad got another job, actually make that two jobs. He got fired from the one at the coffee shop for writing in his journal while serving customers. Some of them complained that he was writing personal stuff about them, and maybe he was. But I can't see how he was hurting anyone. He was doing his job and just trying to stay interested by observing all the little details that go into it. The corporate world would prefer him to be a zombie rather than a thinking, feeling human being.

He's now working at a movie complex, selling popcorn. Believe it or not, he still comes home from work and babbles about how interesting it is. Then he goes upstairs to work on his sequel—Job Book #2. He's one strange dude, but he's my dad.

Then there's Mom. She's still working for the sanitation department in Providence, but she got promoted to an office job. She smells a lot better these days and doesn't have to use nearly as much perfume. But I guess you can take the trash woman out of the truck but you can't take the trash out of her. Every night she still comes home with the little "treasures" she finds after work.

"Look at this," she'll exclaim, emptying her usual bag of junk on the table. "Can you believe someone actually threw this out? John, why don't you try this jacket on? I think I can get that stain out. And Venus, didn't you say you needed a briefcase? It's a little grimy but look, it's got separate compartments and—oops—I guess we can throw away that sandwich."

We've all learned by now to accept Mom's gifts quietly, with a straight face, for we know they come from a messy but loving place deep inside her. It also lends a certain excitement to family dinners. You never quite know what crappy or creepy thing might come pouring out of that bag. And I have to admit, at least the quality of her offerings has been improving. Way to go, Mom!

I do have some good news about one family member, at least I think so. Venus has finally stopped wearing her outfits and spouting about going to Venus someday, though I do kind of miss it sometimes. She hasn't forgotten about her beloved planet. By saving her allowance and with a little help from her grandparents (the ones with the cactus-shaped swimming pool), she bought a powerful telescope complete with a small observatory dome she set up in the backyard. Every clear night she goes out there to observe, filling notebook after notebook with her observations on Venus.

"How can you see anything if it's all surrounded by clouds?" I asked her once. I thought it was a perfectly good question, but she just gave me one of those looks and went back to her telescope. Lately she's gotten so serious that I hardly know her. After dinner she just goes up to her room and works on some new problem in celestial mechanics. She's already been accepted at Brown University, the youngest student ever to qualify for early admission. I do wish she'd recite one of her poems again or maybe put on a sheet and run through the neighborhood so I could protect her from bullies. Or just be silly with me once in a while. I was so busy making fun of her all of the time that I never got to know her other side. I know she is happy in her own way, but I wish she could just laugh or smile to let me know she's still crazy and that everything's OK. I guess I'll just have to wait and see how she turns out.

And then there's Bruno. He seems to grow crazier by the minute. It's almost as if he wants everyone to think he is. He's shaved his hair bald except for a tiny ponytail and wears a black suit, white shirt and tie, and goes door to door through the neighborhood preaching the "Gospel of Bruno" to anyone dumb enough to listen. I think his message has something to do with connecting with your inner musical ecstasy and following the teachings of Hugh Hefner, Howdy Doody, Allen Ginsberg, Gandhi and Uncle Ben, though not necessarily in that order.

At least he hasn't given up on his music, though I must say I prefer the blues he tried to play to the freakish blend of rock, country western, jazz and polka crap he cranks out at all hours from his room each night. "Killer music," he calls it. He's got that right, for nothing grows in our garden anymore and birds fall dead out of the trees.

Bruno's still an animal lover at heart. He's actually read a few veterinary books and has gained enough confidence to operate on various animals in the neighborhood. One night he did surgery on a cat with a brain tumor. I must say, it really brought people together the way they came out, clutching lamps and baseball bats, and surrounding our house while shouting threats above Bruno's music. When the police finally arrived, I was relieved because one guy actually had a gas can and was pointing at our house. But I was also a little sad to see it all end. It's nice to know people can still come out and get excited about things. That's what keeps a neighborhood together. By the way, the cat came out of surgery and is doing quite well, though he has a bad twitch in one eye.

I know Bruno isn't on drugs of any kind, but he certainly acts like he is. He talks complete nonsense in a voice ranging from falsetto to bass tenor. Then he makes his eyes roll and contorts his face as if in pain. I suspect it's all part of his act, for sometimes when we're alone together he acts normal, or at least as normal as Bruno can be. We just talk as brothers, mostly small shit but sometimes big stuff, the kind that matters, like for instance: do you wonder if you'll ever be too old for sex ... or who made God? He may be crazy, but I'm glad he's still here, at least sometimes.

Speaking of crazy, Mary Majello is still with us. Now that she's left her religious order, The Sisters of Creation, we just call her Aunt Mary (or Aunt Jello behind her back). At least she's no longer praying for the cockroaches. Instead she's become a member of the American Anti-Science Libertarian Society. Not only is the group opposed to all laws and government interference with personal liberty but they are also against all so-called laws of nature or science.

I asked her about gravity once, and immediately wished I hadn't. "Why did those scientists have to pass that law?" she asked. "Just think of how much better off the world would be without gravity."

"Aunt Mary, I don't think scientists actually passed it," I tried to explain. "It was more like they discovered it. And science laws are not the same as ..."

"A law is a law, Johnnie boy. First thing they do is pass a law that says everything has to come down so now people are falling off roofs and breaking their bones. I ask you, what would people do if no one had bothered to tell them they had to fall down? Can you imagine? Next thing they'll be passing a law that says things will all come to a stop someday."

"I think we already have that one, Aunt Mary. It's called ..."

"The Second Law of Thermodynamics," said a sarcastic voice from the hallway. "Look it up—you might learn something." It was the first time in a month I'd heard Venus speak. She just shook her head and walked away.

"Well, I never! That girl is so rude. She needs to learn some manners."

Though I was kind of looking forward to a debate, it's probably a good thing that Venus didn't pursue the matter. Aunt Mary is Mom's sister, after all. And lately her behavior seems to be getting more bizarre. Her doctor says she shows signs of dementia and that we should keep a close eye on her. It might have begun sometime in her 50's, though with Aunt Mary even Mom admits it's difficult to know. It's been tough on the family, especially on Mom. Lately, Aunt Mary is convinced that she's being held prisoner in a government concentration camp. Since we started watching her more closely and keeping the doors locked, she assumes we're all guards and is constantly searching for an escape route. One night, after everyone had gone to bed, Mom found her with a pick and crowbar, excavating a tunnel under the living room floor.

"Come to bed, Mary," she said. "This is not a prison."

But Aunt Mary just dropped the pick and held up her hands. "OK, Warden, you win—this time."

The hardest part for Mom is when Aunt Mary forgets Mom's face and name. But then suddenly she'll remember a time when Mom was just a little girl. "Do you remember how you nearly drowned those baby chicks in the rain barrel trying to get them to swim? What a big dope you were!" Then they would just sit and laugh for a while.

It's weird how dementia hits people differently. Take Grandma Geronimo, for instance. We just celebrated her 83rd birthday, and she's still sharp as ever. Of course, there's still that matter of her supposed relationship to Geronimo and her occasional protests at the Federal Building, but she still remembers all our names and is remarkably sharp at recalling family events. In fact, she seems like some wise old medicine woman who knows things about us that no one else knows—a keeper of our family secrets. Sometimes when she's out back in the garden hoeing potatoes,

I'll go and talk to her, especially about our adventure.

"Did it really happen, Grandma? It all seems so unreal. How can a family cease to exist and come back again? Was it all just a story?"

Sitting and pulling her shawl tighter, she rolled a toothpick in her mouth and mumbled. As always, some of her words were completely unintelligible. I think it's some kind of chant she does. But then she came through perfectly clear.

"Johnnie, it's all a story. It's been that way since the beginning of time. Back before Geronimo and before mountains, oceans and rivers and before even the earth and the stars, there was always the story. It is a story that lives in our hearts. You must hold fast to your family memories, Johnnie, for they are spirits that will guide you in this life and whatever comes after. They are as much a part of you as your flesh and bones. Don't be impatient with your family, for like you they are still in a process of becoming. We are all headed to that same unknowable blackness in space and time, and we need to hold on for all we're worth. Just like we did in our story. Yes, it *was* real. And the only reason we didn't cease to exist is because we all believed in each other. You must never forget us, Johnnie."

Grandma Geronimo touched my face and smiled a toothless grin. "You're the new keeper of the family now. Guard us well." Then she sighed and leaned back against her favorite sycamore tree, and closed her eyes as if she were taking a nap. It happened so peacefully that it was minutes before I knew she was gone.

We all knew she would leave us someday, but it still took us by surprise. I don't think any of realized just how much her special brand of craziness helped keep us together. And though we all grieved for a time, her death was such a quiet and natural thing that it was more like the gentle passing of a rain shower that left us feeling curiously refreshed.

Of course, she isn't really gone. Lately, she's all I've been writing about. Her memory keeps getting stronger in me every day. Mom has helped fill in a lot of the details, and I've even discovered some genealogical stuff at the library that proves she really did have a little of Geronimo's blood in her veins.

As for the rest of our story, it's like the book of life, as Grandma used to say. Life just keeps on going, evolving into ever newer and sometimes weirder forms. And making lots of mistakes along the way in becoming whatever it will.

Speaking of mistakes, Grandma was the only one in our family willing to talk about our little trip. Everyone else refuses to acknowledge that something really happened to us, as if it were just some kind of bad dream. Whenever I mention "the story," they just change the subject and give me a desperate look. I wonder what they're thinking. Do they still blame me for what I put them through? I mean, what kind of guy writes his whole family away? I never meant to do such a thing—at least I don't think so. It was just a writing game, like the "vacations" I used to take in my imagination. One thing I have learned, though: words are powerful stuff. You think that just because you arrange and compose them on the page you still have control over them. But once you set them into motion, words have a life all their own. No telling where they might go. Sometimes they'll take you to places strange and wonderful. And sometimes they'll take you to places all too real and terrifying. I never knew writing could be so dangerous. Guess I'll have to be more careful.

Grandma also helped me to understand and deal with my own brand of craziness. She taught me that we're all a little crazy in one way or another—that's part of what makes us human. The trick is in recognizing these little quirks or flaws in ourselves and in others, and finding ways to make them work for you.

Though our family still has its share of crazy moments, things don't seem quite as absurd as before. I can't say whether it's me or them. Maybe I've finally learned a little wisdom and appreciate them more (or not!).

Or maybe they're all still wondering about what happened and if it might happen again. Things do seem a bit dull around here. Our family story doesn't seem to be going anywhere lately. I've been thinking a lot about what will happen to us in the future. Who knows how we'll turn out? Meanwhile, I'll just wait and watch and record.

I almost miss our little adventure. While I'm waiting, maybe I could add a few details, you know just tweak the plot a little. Perhaps add a few new family members.

Just kidding, of course. Don't want to go *there* again. One crazy family is more than enough for anyone.

LaVergne, TN USA
14 September 2010
197027LV00001B/22/P